DIAL BOOKS
An imprint of Penguin Group (USA) Inc.
Published by The Penguin Group
Penguin Group (USA) Inc., 375 Hudson Street, New York, New York 10014, U.S.A.

Penguin Group (Canada), 90 Eglinton Avenue East, Suite 700, Toronto, Ontario, Canada M4P 2Y3
(a division of Pearson Penguin Canada Inc.) • Penguin Books Ltd, 80 Strand, London WC2R 0RL,
England • Penguin Ireland, 25 St Stephen's Green, Dublin 2, Ireland (a division of Penguin Books
Ltd) • Penguin Group (Australia), 250 Camberwell Road, Camberwell, Victoria 3124, Australia (a
division of Pearson Australia Group Pty Ltd) • Penguin Books India Pvt Ltd, 11 Community Centre,
Panchsheel Park, New Delhi - 110 017, India • Penguin Group (NZ), 67 Apollo Drive, Rosedale,
Auckland 0632, New Zealand (a division of Pearson New Zealand Ltd.) • Penguin Books (South
Africa) (Pty) Ltd, 24 Sturdee Avenue, Rosebank, Johannesburg 2196, South Africa • Penguin Books Ltd,
Registered Offices: 80 Strand, London WC2R 0RL, England

This book is a work of fiction. Names, characters, places, and incidents are either the product
of the author's imagination or are used fictitiously, and any resemblance to actual persons,
living or dead, business establishments, events, or locales is entirely coincidental.

CIP Data is available.

Published in the United States by Dial Books
An imprint of Penguin Group (USA) Inc.
345 Hudson Street, New York, New York 10014
www.penguin.com/youngreaders

Designed by Nancy R. Leo-Kelly
Text set in Dante
Printed in U. S. A.
10 9 8 7 6 5 4 3 2 1

ISBN 978-0-8037-3721-1

love?
maybe.

Heather Hepl

Dial

an imprint of Penguin Group (USA

♡ ♡ ♡
For my dad who taught me to work hard,
love long, and forgive easily.
And as always for Harrison.
Thank you for making my life so sweet.

love?
maybe.

chapter ONE

Claire tells me it's romantic that my birthday is on Valentine's Day, but then she thinks it's romantic when Stuart remembers to say excuse me after he burps. Jillian tells me it's unfortunate, but only because she thinks it lowers the gift receiving opportunities. I don't really care one way or the other. February 14th has always been just another day to me.

"All I'm saying is that we need a plan," Jillian says. I nod without looking up.

"Yes, but why are you saying this to *me*?" I ask.

"Because you have a plan for everything," Jillian says, pointing to my date book, lying open on the counter. In between customers, I was trying to work out my semester. But right now I'm trying to finish stocking the front case before I have to leave. It's not as easy as it looks, building pyramids out of round chocolates. One misplaced candy and you have an avalanche.

"Fine," I say, giving in to Jillian. "Tell me the plan."

"Well, I don't have the whole thing worked out yet," she says. "That's where you and your compulsive organizational skills come in." I roll my eyes. She nudges me, making me knock over a pile of coconut truffles. "Sorry," she says, making big eyes at me. I sigh and start building again. "The first step is getting you to admit that we need a plan."

I have to stifle the urge to roll my eyes again. Ever since Jan hung the big pink hearts in the window and started playing Sinatra *all the time*, Jillian's been obsessed with finding a boyfriend. Thankfully I don't have to participate that much in her lunacy. She's like a windup toy; all I have to do is nod and um-hum in the appropriate places to keep her going. I look over at Claire for help, but she's tapping away on her phone. Texting Stuart, no doubt. I keep stacking the truffles. I think the coconut ones are completely nasty, but they're one of our biggest sellers.

"I still don't see what the big deal is," I say. I sneak a look at Jillian out of the corner of my eye. She's staring at me, her mouth slightly open, like I just told her I didn't see what the big deal is with oxygen. "I mean, it's not like it's the end of the world if you don't have a boyfriend for Valentine's Day." Jillian actually turns away from me as if I offended her.

"Did you hear that?" she asks Claire.

Claire looks up from her phone slowly. "Hear what?"

Jillian shakes her head. "Good thing you two have me," she says.

"We are very lucky," I say dutifully. Either Jillian doesn't hear the sarcasm in my voice or she chooses to ignore it. I can't tell. "Any word from Stuart?" I ask, looking over at Claire. She shakes her head. "Maybe he doesn't have phone service up in the mountains." I feel my heart start racing like it always does when I lie.

"Maybe," Claire says, but I don't think she believes it any more than I do. Stuart's on a family ski trip. He's only been gone four days, but to look at Claire, you'd think it was four hundred. In the year Claire and Stuart have been together, I don't think they have gone more than eight hours without talking to each other and that's just because they have to sleep. But in the last month or so, he's been acting squirrelly. And the weirder he acts, the clingier Claire gets. And the more freaked out Claire gets, the more Stuart seems to retreat. I've noticed he keeps looking behind him when they're together, like he's searching for an exit. I've seen the signs before. So his silence is a bit ominous.

Jan pushes through the door to the kitchen, balancing a long metal tray covered in foil in his hands. "Coming through," he says, stepping up beside me. He places the tray on the counter in front of me. Even though he does it gently, it sends the coconut truffles I just stacked spinning off in a dozen different directions. Jan looks at me sheepishly, but I just sigh. He nods at the tray in front of us. "Let the guessing begin," he says. "Piper, you first."

I pretend to think for a moment. "Chocolate," I say, teasing him.

Jan sighs. "At least try," he says.

"Milk chocolate."

He shakes his head and points at Jillian. "Your turn."

"Strawberries and Cream," she says, trying to peek under the foil. Jan pushes her hand away and shakes his head.

"Cupid's Crunch," Claire says, picking up her phone and checking it for the five thousandth time.

"No, but points for creativity," Jan says. "Give up?" He smiles, pinching the corner of the foil with his fingers, ready to whip it off and reveal the new flavor of truffle. This is his favorite moment. He changes the featured flavor out every month. Sometimes it's good, like Mocha Caramel Madness. Sometimes boring, like Mango. Sometimes weird, like Chipotle Banana. Once just plain gross, like last summer when Jan decided to try making avocado candies. Even dubbing them Green Goddess hadn't gotten many to sample them.

"We give up," I say. Jan whips off the foil, revealing dozens of brown balls with purple squiggles all over them. No one says anything, making Claire get up and walk over to look at the pan too. "What is it?" I ask, trying to smell anything unusual.

"Kalamata Caramel," Jan says. "Awesome, right?" He looks from Jillian to me to Claire, a big smile on his face.

"Awesome," I say, hoping I sound more enthusiastic than I feel.

"Wait, you mean Kalamata *olives*?" Jillian asks.

"Yep," Jan says, clearly excited. "Of course, I just used the olive juice, not the actual olives."

Jillian nods, her face unreadable. "Good call," she says. Claire nods in agreement. "Okay, I'll try one." Jillian picks up a truffle and pops it in her mouth. She closes her eyes for a moment, chewing. Then her eyes pop open. "These are good," she says, reaching for another. "Really good." Jan just smiles and nods toward Claire and me. Claire takes one, but I reach under the counter for a rag and the box of chalk.

"I'll make the sign," I say, trying to get away before Jan asks me to try one and I have to give him my honest opinion. I am all about the truth. Not so much because I'm overly moral, but because I am the world's worst liar. I stutter. I start sweating. My pupils dilate. I get this twitchy thing in my left eye. Besides, I'm really not the best at judging Jan's creations. As weird as it sounds, I just don't like chocolate very much. I'm pretty sure the addition of olives isn't going to change that.

Jillian and Claire follow me outside to the sidewalk. They sit at one of the tables Jan has out front, right in front of the lettering on the window. JAN THE CANDY MAN. Although

7

it's not yet lunchtime, people are already starting to filter into the store for their sweet fix. That's one thing about Jan's: Even the most hard-core health fanatics can find something they'll want to buy, even if it's just the homemade granola Jan makes.

The blackboard out front still features January's flavor: Pineapple Orange Banana, or Pine-or-ban as Jan calls it. Surprisingly, it was a big seller. Several people even started stopping by for a quarter pound first thing in the morning. I'm pretty sure that even though it has fruit and milk in it, it still isn't breakfast.

When I first started working here about a year and a half ago, I thought it was Jan's crazy ideas that were keeping his store from getting the attention it should have, but now I know it's not his candy making. Jan's a culinary genius. Somehow he puts weird things together and they taste amazing. Jan's big problem is organization. That's where I come in.

For January I drew the three fruits playing instruments; the pineapple on drums, the orange with a saxophone, and the banana on vocals, of course. Sort of a tropical jazz trio. I use the rag to clean the blackboard. Then I start drawing olives waltzing with what I hope look like caramels.

"We need a plan," Jillian says for the seven thousandth time this morning.

"You've said." I use a piece of coppery chalk to color in the caramels.

"We need three reasonably good-looking, moderately interesting, not utterly hopeless guys."

"Two," Claire says. Jillian stares at her and I say a silent prayer that for once Jillian will be slightly sympathetic.

"Okay, two. Two decent guys in all of Atlanta. That shouldn't be too hard."

I look past Jillian and smile. "I think fate just smiled on you." She looks around then quickly snaps her head back to glare at me. "Hey, Jeremy," I say to the guy walking up behind her. Jillian stares holes into my face before reaching into her purse and pulling out her sunglasses.

Jeremy barely nods in my direction. "Hi, Jillian," he says. I wince as his voice cracks in the middle. Jillian hardly acknowledges him. He stands there for a couple of moments, hopeful. I can't help but feel sorry for the guy. He is head over heels in love with Jillian, but at best she seems to tolerate him. Just another in a long line of examples of why love is so stupid. Finally Jeremy walks past and slips into Jan's.

"Okay," I say when the door shuts behind him. "One down." I'm pretty sure Jillian is glaring at me, but it's hard to tell with her dark glasses.

"Yeah, um, Germy doesn't count," she says.

"But he likes you," I say.

"Piper, please be serious." I look over at Claire and see she's smiling, so I keep going.

"But, just think, Jillian, he'd probably name a character after you in Warcraft," I say.

♥ love? maybe.

"Maybe he'd play you a song on his clarinet," Claire says. Jillian sighs.

"Okay," I say, adding curlicues around the edges of the blackboard. "I'll be serious."

"I'm just tired of being single," Jillian says. "And Piper, aren't you ready? I mean, you haven't really dated anyone since what's-his-name last fall."

"Eric," I say, coloring the olives deep purple. "His name was Eric. But he doesn't count. That was under duress." Claire rolls her eyes. Eric is Stuart's wingman—something he actually calls himself, which should have been a clue. I went out with him once because Claire begged me to. It was awesome. When it's humid, my purple hoodie still smells vaguely of vomit. "Wait," I say, smiling. "You're forgetting Peter."

"You only went out with Peter like three times," Jillian says.

"True. And they were also under duress."

"Stop using that word," Jillian says. "It's not like anyone forced you to go out with him."

"Seriously?" I can't keep my indignation to myself. "Jillian, when you begged me to go with you to *accidentally bump into* Mike VanSickle at Zuzu's, you neglected to mention that you had actually already told Mike you'd swing by *and* that you'd bring a friend. What do you call that?"

Jillian rolls her eyes at me. "Well, that was the one time, but you also went with him to the ASPCA Day in the Park."

I take a deep breath and count to ten. Backwards. Slowly. "Only because you kept telling me that for every ten dollars the animal shelter raised, the life of a puppy would be saved!"

"And you watched a movie together," she says.

I don't bother responding. I've already told her about watching half a movie with Peter because I couldn't stand to sit through the whole thing.

"What exactly do you have against dating anyway?" Jillian asks.

I shrug. "I just don't see the point. It's not like it's required."

"Piper, please," Jillian says, dismissing Eric, Peter, my arguments, and the last of my sanity with the flip of her fingers. "I'm just saying. It's time."

"Time," I say, looking at my watch. "I have to go. I'm supposed to be at my mom's shop in ten minutes." I stare at my drawing of waltzing caramels and olives. It's missing something. I decide to give top hats to the olives and high heels to the caramels and quickly sketch them in.

"Go," Claire says. "We'll finish up." I give her a grateful smile and untie my apron. I pull the door to the shop open and holler to Jan, who has disappeared into the back.

"Jan," I say, balling up my apron and lobbing it toward the bin under the counter. "I have to go."

He peeks his head out. "Thanks for the help, Piper. See you in a few days?"

"I have to check with my mom. I'll call you." He nods and

smiles, his eyes crinkling under his wire-rimmed glasses. I think I've gotten away, but Jan hurries over to me, and thrusts a paper bag into my hands. "Don't forget your candy," he says. "I want your honest opinion."

"Thanks," I say, taking the bag. I kick myself for not getting out of there faster. I step back outside. "Bye!" I yell, tearing past Claire and Jillian as they finish coloring my drawing.

"Don't be late tomorrow!" Claire yells.

"I won't!" I yell over my shoulder, laughing. Claire likes to tease me about my punctuality. I am always early for everything.

I'm sort of proud of myself for actually being able to run the whole way over to my mom's shop. Maybe the fact that I'm not totally sucking O's by the time I get there means that the first day of swim practice won't be horrible. I pause and check out my appearance in one of the big windows on the front of the store. I can half see myself, with my cutoffs and rainbow checked Vans and my T-shirt from last year's regional meet. But I can also half see through the window into my mom's flower shop, so that on top of my usual stick-straight brown hair, I have a vase of purple tulips coming out of my head. It's weird for sure, but a definite improvement over the usual Piper. The door opens and my mother pokes her head out.

"There you are! You're right on time—" The rest of whatever she says disappears into the shop with her. I walk over, catch the door before it closes, and follow her in. With a bang, my little brother, Dominic, tears out of the workroom with my little sister, Lucy, close behind. She chases him around the shop with a leftover sprig of mistletoe held out in front of her. She's making kissing noises as she runs. Each time she starts to close in on Dominic, he screams and bolts away again. They careen past, bouncing off me and into a low table full of African violets, knocking several pots onto their sides. As soon as they see me, they're on me, or rather on the bag I'm carrying.

"Candy!" They both shriek.

"No screaming please," my mother says. She relieves them of the bag with promises that they can each have *one* after dinner if they are good. *Fat chance.* "Piper's here to take you home!" She says it in her bouncy, happy voice. It's the same voice she uses for everything she thinks might get an argument: cleaning the litter box, getting shots at the doctor, eating Brussels sprouts. It only takes a few minutes to get Dom and Lucy rounded up and out the door. My mother is taking an order on the phone as we leave, but she offers me a grateful smile and mouths thank you.

I follow Lucy and Dom down the sidewalk toward Commerce Avenue. We've been spending a lot of time together over the last couple weeks. With Valentine's Day roses, Easter lilies, and then the march of the June weddings, this is the start of a busy time of year for florists. Mostly I don't mind helping out, but occasionally I miss the days when I was an only child. The peace and quiet and first dibs on the bathroom were nice.

We are home exactly four minutes (I know this because that's the amount of time necessary to microwave two bowls of Easy Mac) when the kitchen sink explodes. No—really. Suddenly there is water everywhere. I try to turn off the miniature geyser that is erupting from the faucet, but twisting the knobs doesn't help. I start digging cleaning supplies out from under the sink and find the water valves below. Living in an old building has made me pretty handy. I manage to shut off the water, but not before I am thoroughly drenched and there is a good inch of water on the kitchen floor.

"Whoa," Dominic says from the doorway. He begins jumping up and down in the puddle, sending streams of water everywhere.

"Stop," I yell, running for the hall closet. I pull out a stack of beach towels and head back to the kitchen. My wet socks leave a trail across the living room floor. I notice that Lucy has left her spot in front of the television and joined Dom in the kitchen. Sighing in defeat, I watch them splash for a while, grateful that it's just water spraying the cabinets and not ketchup like last time.

Once they've worn themselves out, I hand them each a towel and make them help me clean up the mess. Of course, this is a mixed bag because soon Dom is snapping his wet towel at Lucy and she's screaming at him to stop. I finally get them settled in front of cartoons with a bowl each of pasta covered in a sauce so orange that I'm pretty sure it glows in the dark.

Just half an hour until bedtime. I keep repeating this to myself.

I take our recycling bin out to the curb for pickup. I take a deep breath of the night air, savoring the quiet. Mr. Wishman, from next door, is just setting his recycling out, too. Their dog, Duncan, runs circles around his legs. I wave hello and start to ask him when Charlie is getting back, but I guess he doesn't hear me because he quickly heads back inside, Duncan following close at his heels.

I walk back into the house and peek at Dom and Lucy, who are thankfully still parked in front of cartoons. I return to the kitchen and pull out the jar of peanut butter and a spoon. Gross, I know, but whatever. I'm just about to take my first bite when the phone rings. (Jillian wonders how I stay so thin. Big secret: no time to eat.)

"Hello?" All I can hear is sniffling. Then my name, soft and watery.

"Claire?" More sniffling.

"He still hasn't called." Another sniff. "Why hasn't he called?" I look up at the ceiling. Here is where things get tricky. Do I tell her he's probably just busy or out of range? Or do I tell her what I'm pretty sure she already suspects. I mean, I like Stuart in general, but he's never really been the great guy that Claire thinks he is.

There's really no choice. Even over the phone, I'm a terrible liar. "Claire, I think—"

"Pipe, I gotta go. Stuart's on the other line. See you tomorrow." She's gone before I can even say good-bye. I want to tell her to stop being so available, to stop making herself nuts over him, but then I don't even pretend to know what love feels like. I sigh and put my phone back on the counter. Hopefully Stuart has an awesome excuse, like he fell off the ski lift and is in a full body cast. Or maybe he'll just tell Claire the truth. I won't hold my breath for either.

"Dom! Luce! Let's get cleaned up for bed." I brace myself for the tears and the begging, but instead they're totally quiet. With them, quiet means trouble. I walk into the living room and see Dom holding Miss Kitty, our fifteen-year-old cat, on his lap while Lucy uses a purple Sharpie to draw curlicues all over her white fur. Mac and cheese, love-struck friends, a tattooed cat, and an exploding sink. Just another day in the life of Piper Paisley.

chapter **two**

Just one more chapter?" Lucy begs.

"No," I say. "You have to get to sleep."

"Mom always reads us two," Dom says.

He's right. "Okay, one more and then bed." They both nod. I settle back into the beanbag. At this rate, I'll never get my English paper finished. I hate admitting it, but sometimes I resent my mom for dumping all of this on me. But then I'll look at Lucy's sweet smile, or Dom will say something that makes me laugh harder than I can ever remember laughing and I'll feel really lucky to be so close to them. That is, until they do something awful, like shaking up a can of soda and opening it just to see how far it will spray. (The answer is all over my laptop.)

I finally get Lucy and Dom to bed with promises to send Mom up when she gets home. Feeling sticky-nasty from chocolates, cheese sauce, and the four spoonfuls of peanut butter that were my dinner, I decide on a shower. I stand under the hot water until I realize it's making me sleepy. Knowing I still have about two hours of homework in front of me, I twist the knob, sending cold water raining down on me. I have to stifle a scream. It's horrible, but it does the trick. I am definitely awake.

I hurry into my pajamas, trying to make my teeth stop chattering. I drag my newly refurbished laptop onto the bed and open a new file. I stare at the blinking cursor until it threatens to hypnotize me. I have to write five to seven pages of brilliance and I can't even come up with a title for my paper. "Focus," I tell myself. If I can't finish this paper tonight, I'm going to have to rework my schedule for the rest of the week. I rub my eyes, trying to concentrate, but then I hear a noise on the roof.

Normally, noises on roofs scare people, but not me. A noise on my roof means one of two things: Either the ginormous pecan tree out front has finally fallen on the house like my stepfather, Beau, always worries it will—and come on, that's never going to happen—or it means that Charlie's home.

There's another big bump on the roof above my head. I quickly hop out of bed and grab a sweatshirt from my closet. I hurry to the window and open it. A blast of cold air hits me hard, making me gasp. My room is the smallest one in the house, but what it lacks in size, it more than makes up for with access to the roof. I grab the chocolates Jan gave me (minus the two I gave to Lucy and Dom) from my desk and climb out on my windowsill, using the trellis to hoist myself up. My mother would freak if she knew I was up here. But I'm such a good daughter ninety-nine percent of the time that I figure I'm allowed this one bit of rebellion.

"Hey," I say into the dark. "When'd you get home?"

"Couple of hours ago."

I smile toward the dark shape outlined against the sky. Charlie and I have been friends ever since his family moved in next door nearly eight years ago. I walk over and sit beside him, hooking my heels on the gutter.

"Here," I say, sliding the bag of chocolates over toward him. "I can't promise anything."

"Oh man, I was hoping—" He opens the bag and pops one of the truffles into his mouth. I hear him chewing and then silence. "Um, Piper?"

"Kalamata Caramel," I say.

"As in olives?"

"Yep," I say, trying hard not to laugh. I couldn't bring myself to try them.

"Huh," he says, popping another one in his mouth. "Actually, they're pretty good." Charlie puts the bag down on the roof between us.

"Dom and Lucy liked it," I say. "Of course, I didn't tell them they were olive flavored."

"Did *you* make these?"

"No," I say. "I don't think in a million years I would have guessed that olives and caramel might taste good together." But that's why Jan's the artist and I'm the bookkeeper. Six months ago, Jan did finally get me to make something. He helped me create a whole line of unusual taffy flavors. At first it was just the underappreciated fruit flavors like plum and cantaloupe. Then I really started branching out. The breakfast collection (flavors included bacon, orange juice, and pancake) was mentioned in the *Atlanta Journal-Constitution* last fall along with the Readers' Picks. Jan was really proud of me. The added exposure, along with the new Flavor of the Month truffles, helped earn Jan's the title of Best Candy in Atlanta. My mom's flower shop was named the Best Florist for the third year in a row.

"So what do you have brewing for Valentine's this year?" Charlie asks.

"Well—" I pause for dramatic effect. "Consternation Hearts." Charlie doesn't say anything. "You know, like conversation hearts—but instead of I Love You or Say Yes, mine say Buzz Off and No Way."

"Pretty clever," Charlie says.

"I know, right?" I say. Charlie shakes his head. We sit there looking out at the lights of the city and the handful of stars you can see from in town. "How was your trip?' I ask finally.

"Okay," he says.

"Okay? What about all those California girls you were talking about before you left?"

"Well, that part was pretty good," he says.

"Heartbreaker," I say.

Charlie puts up his hand. "No hearts were broken."

"How was it with your mom?" I ask.

"Weird," he says. Charlie's dad and mom split up at the end of last summer and his mom moved out to California. This was his first trip to see her.

"Weird how?" I ask.

"Just weird seeing her without my dad, you know?" I nod. I'm familiar with that kind of weirdness, having lived through my mom's two divorces.

"Tell me it gets easier," he says. I can't see his face in the darkness, but I can hear the sadness in his voice.

"It gets easier," I say, but I can't really muster any conviction. It took me a long time to get used to seeing my mom with Beau and it's never been easy seeing her without him.

"The truth, Piper," he says.

"It stinks," I say.

"Yeah, it does." We sit like that for a few more minutes, just watching the twinkling lights from downtown. "So how's it going with Pete?" Charlie asks.

"You really *have* been gone awhile."

"Already?" Charlie asks. "I thought he'd at least make it through the end of the month."

"Had to cut him loose," I say.

"Why did you agree to go out with him anyway? I thought you had a no-dating policy."

I sigh. "I thought maybe it wouldn't be awful."

"Well, what did him in?" Charlie asks. "Bad breath? Cold hands?"

I shake my head. "We were watching *The Day the Earth Stood Still*. But instead of calling the guardian a robot, he kept calling it a row-butt."

"So you broke up with him because he mispronounced a word?" Charlie shakes his head. "Harsh."

"I was nice," I say. "I just told him we probably shouldn't see each other anymore."

"On account of his row-butt."

"Exactly."

Charlie shakes his head again. "Harsh."

"Harsh? At least I was honest. Guys just sort of evaporate," I say, thinking of Stuart. Charlie doesn't have a response to that.

"Hey, I brought you something," he says. "Close your eyes." I do, listening to the rustle of plastic, and then silence. "Okay," he says. I open my eyes to see Charlie holding what looks like a heart, but not a Valentine's Day heart. A real heart.

"Eww," I say, poking at the heart-shaped blob in his hand. It's not solid, but made out of silicone, so it even feels like a real heart. Or what I imagine one would feel like. "It's awesome," I say, poking it again.

Charlie shrugs and hands the heart to me. It feels cool against my hand. "I know you collect them." I laugh. What

Charlie really knows is that I definitely *do not* collect them. It's more like other people collect them for me. Because my birthday is on Valentine's Day, everyone gives me things with hearts on them. However, this is the first anatomically correct heart I've ever gotten.

I look over at Charlie, but he's staring up at the sky. "Make a wish," he says, pointing above us. I look up just in time to see the falling star. "What did you wish for?" he asks, looking at me.

"I can't tell you," I say.

"Afraid it won't come true?" he asks.

"Well, duh," I say.

"I should go," he says, standing up and brushing off the back of his shorts. "I still have to finish my trig and my chem lab write-up." Charlie doesn't go to the private school I attend. He goes to public, but he's in all the honors classes, which means he usually has as much or more homework than I do.

"I'm slammed too," I say. I stand up and start making my way back toward my window, catching the edge of the roof in my hand.

"Stop by tomorrow after school," I say.

"Can't," he says. "I have practice." Charlie is totally dedicated to swimming. Most of the time his hair is slightly greenish and he reeks of chlorine.

"Friday then." Charlie mumbles something as he hops across to his roof. "I'll bring chocolate."

"I'm there," he says, ducking inside. He sticks his head out. "Can you get Jan to make some Peanuttiest truffles?"

I laugh. "I'll see what I can do." I climb back into my room, closing my window tight behind me. I lay my heart on my desk, smiling as it quivers when I release it. Yuck.

I climb back onto my bed and pull my comforter around me, trying to get warm. I stare at my laptop. I give up after my eyes start blurring again. I decide to get some sleep and get up extra early in the morning to work. I set my alarm for 4:30 and climb under the covers.

I lie there thinking about Claire and Stuart and Dom and Lucy and poor Miss Kitty. I think about how tired my mom must be and olive candies. I think about The Plan and Jillian's assertion that we need one. And I think about how I lied to Charlie. It's not that I'm afraid my wish won't come true if I tell him what it is. It's that I didn't make one. I don't believe in wishes. Wishes make you hopeful and being hopeful is just a big setup for disappointment.

chapter **three**

I wake up when I hear my mom calling up the stairs. The first thing I notice is that it's already light out. The second thing I notice is that the numbers on my clock are blinking at me.

I curse, kicking my covers off. Stinking power outage. I hurry into the bathroom, stubbing my toe on the corner of the door. I cuss again, but then regret it when I see Dom poking his head out of his room.

"Mommy!" Dom calls. "Piper said a bad word." I shoot him a dirty look, then hustle Lucy out of the bathroom and shut the door before I can hear my mother's response. The good news is my hair is clean. The bad news is I slept on it wet and now half of it is plastered to the side of my head and the other half is sticking straight out to the side, giving me a weird bird of paradise look. I ignore the knock at the door.

I brush my hair, trying to make both sides look even, but all I manage to do is make it all a big mess. There's another knock. I pull a headband out of the drawer and slip it on. A little better. There is another knock.

"Lucy!" I yank the door open. "Can't you see—" It's not Lucy at the door, but my mother. She tilts her head at me.

"Are you okay?" she asks.

"Super," I say, stepping past her. I clomp into my room but stop as soon as I see the bed. Not only is my bed made, but there is a big stack of folded, clean clothes piled at the end of it. I turn to look at my mother. "Thanks," I say, feeling about an inch tall.

"It's nothing," she says. She turns to tie a ribbon to Lucy's ponytail before shooing her downstairs. It's not nothing and I know it. There's no telling how late my mother stayed up last night doing laundry, and if the smell of bacon wafting up the stairs is real, there's no telling how early she got up to make breakfast.

I grab my uniform, which I note is not only clean, but ironed. My mother is combing Dom's hair. He stands completely still while she does it, which is a miracle because when I come at him with a brush, he runs screaming away from me. My mother shooshes him downstairs and then turns to me. She raises her eyebrows, still holding the brush in her hand. Normally I wouldn't dream of letting my mother touch my hair, but my guilt and the fact that my hair can't get any worse make me nod. I have to bend to allow her to reach the top of my head. I passed her height-wise about a year ago. Now I have about three inches on her and I'm showing no sign of slowing down.

"Thanks," I say when she finishes. She smiles and hands me the brush.

"Hurry, so you can eat before you go." I nod. She pulls my door shut as she leaves. Breakfast. Novel concept. I get dressed fast, frowning at the tiny run in my tights. I peek in the mirror before heading downstairs. My mother managed to twist my hair into this complicated-looking knot at the back of my head. It feels like my eyebrows are being pulled up to the top of my head, but I have to admit it looks pretty good.

I know I'm making a pig of myself at breakfast, but it's the first meal I can remember in the last week that didn't: a) come from a vending machine, b) come from a delivery person, and/or c) have enough chemicals in it to actually change my molecular blueprint. Dom and Lucy keep interrupting each other to talk to my mother. She laughs when Dom tells her about jumping in the water all over the kitchen floor. Yes, my life is just one big comedy show.

"How about you, Piper?" my mother asks. She takes a sip of her coffee and looks at me.

I shrug, trying to think of something interesting to say. "Claire finally heard from Stuart last night."

"Poor Claire," my mother says. I notice she didn't even ask what they talked about. I guess as the leavee instead of the leaver of two marriages, my mother just assumes that Stuart broke it off with Claire.

Mom sighs and pushes away from the table. "I'd better get a shower," she says, standing up. She walks around the table, kissing each of us on the head before heading toward the stairs. "Thank you for taking them to school."

"No problem," I say.

"Once we get through Valentine's Day, things will mellow out." I nod. Even though I sometimes feel put out with all the stuff I have to do around the house, I know my mom's slammed at work and I know she wishes it could be different. "Be good for Piper," she says to Dom and Lucy. They smile at her like angels. More like angels with their halos stapled to their horns.

I wolf down another piece of bacon before getting up and putting my dishes in the sink. I look from Dom to Lucy. "Stay put," I say, heading upstairs. Halfway through brushing my teeth, I hear screaming downstairs.

"Piper!"

I grab my backpack and shove my laptop inside. I hear the shower running and my mother singing as I pass the bathroom. Another scream. I hurry down the stairs, bracing myself for whatever is going on down there. I round the corner, my mouth already open, preparing to yell, but both Lucy and Dom are sitting at the table right where I left them. I quickly look around the room, trying to figure out what happened while I was gone, but then I see the clock.

"Arrggghhh!" I yell. I'm going to be late. I shove my arms into my coat and twist my scarf around my neck. I hunt for a few moments for my left penny loafer. I finally give up and shove my feet into my flowered rain boots. I shepherd both Lucy and Dom in front of me and out the door. It isn't until I'm just about to pull the door shut behind me that I see the reason for all the screaming. Swimming in the aquarium with the fish is my missing left shoe.

"Why didn't you call me?" Claire whispers as I slide into my seat. My boots squeak against the linoleum. I had hoped to enter unnoticed, but Mr. Reyes spotted me as I was coming in, earning me a dirty look and probably a detention.

"I just got your message," I say. After dropping off Dom and Lucy, I checked my cell. **Call me. v.v. urgent!!! C.** I look over at Claire. Her eyes are red and watery. "Are you okay?" I whisper, but she just shakes her head and looks at her desk.

I put my head down on my arms. Despite the fact that I overslept or maybe because of it, I feel exhausted, like even my bones are tired. Mr. Reyes makes the usual announcements. It's one of the high points of the day for many people. We're allowed to write our own announcements.

The bell finally rings and I pick up my book bag, staggering under the weight of three textbooks, two novels, one laptop, assorted pens and highlighters, a calculator, and a slightly bruised apple that I added on the way out of the house. Mr.

Reyes is busy with someone else as I pass his desk, allowing me to slip out without a detention—at least for now.

"Tell me," I say to Claire as she follows me to my locker.

"It's Stuart," she says. I raise my eyebrows, not sure what to say. "He said he thinks we should have a little space."

She looks at me for a long moment. I take a deep breath. "You did say last semester that you wondered what it would be like to go out with someone else." I realize too late that I've said the exact wrong thing. Claire's eyes spill over. I offer her a very crumpled napkin from my bag. She takes it and blows her nose. I pull my locker open. I roll my eyes when I see the bottle of purple nail polish sitting in front of my books.

"Is it supposed to rain today?" a voice behind me asks. I turn and see Jillian walking toward us and staring pointedly at my galoshes.

"From you?" I ask, holding up the bottle of nail polish. Jillian shrugs. She's always leaving her little "self-improvement" tools in my locker. Jillian looks over at Claire and raises an eyebrow. "Let me guess," she says. "You heard from Stuart." Claire nods, then blows her nose into the paper napkin I gave her. I scrounge in my locker for the pair of flats I was sure I left there last week. I finally give up, resigning myself to a day of sweaty feet. Double awesome.

"I need some sugar and caffeine," I say, thinking maybe a couple of cookies and an Americano might clear the fog covering my brain. I push my locker closed. We start heading toward the cafeteria, weaving in between the clusters of people standing around the halls. The administration has threatened a bazillion times to get rid of morning break, saying it cuts into learning time, but I'm pretty sure they'd have a minor rebellion on their hands if they actually did. And not just from the students. Right after homeroom all the teachers make a dash for the teachers' lounge. I had to go in there once to pick up a book for my lit class. All the teachers were standing around pounding coffee and stuffing themselves full of donuts. They were like wild animals at the kill. I got out of there as quickly as I could, careful not to turn my back to them. Who knew if they would mistake me as being jelly-filled?

The caff is packed. We get in line behind a cluster of senior girls who look at us like we're offensive, which in my case might actually be true considering how my boots are making my feet sweat like crazy. And with Claire sniffling like she's got the plague, it's no wonder they push forward to give us a little more room. When we get up to the counter, I grab a cinnamon roll. One look at Claire and I take a second one. If anyone is in need of some raw sugar, it's her. Jillian picks up a carton of yogurt and we slide down the line toward the coffee. By all accounts, our school is pretty plush. Not too many high schools have a cappuccino machine and a sushi bar.

We pay and make our way over to one of the tables. I slide into a chair near the window and immediately tuck into the

cinnamon roll. Jillian is watching me. She seems slightly horrified by me. I often catch her looking at me like I'm something stuck to the bottom of her shoe. I guess because she's
very image conscious. Somehow she manages to make even
the basic uniform stylish. I'm not that into fashion and hair
and I never wear makeup.

"Look, Claire," Jillian finally says, tearing her eyes away
from the train wreck that is apparently me. "Prince Charming Stuart was not." She's about as compassionate as a bull-
dozer. "You're just going to have to get back on the horse."
I point out she only just fell off the horse yesterday. Jillian
nods. "But it's not like we didn't see this coming," she says.
Claire stares at me. I have to nod. Darn truth.

"He said he needs to focus on himself for a while," Claire
says. I don't know what to say to that. As far as I know Stuart's
always been pretty good at taking care of Stuart.

"Stuart is a moron," Jillian says. Claire gives her a smile,
making me feel vaguely like a failure. Here I sit, Claire's best
friend since elementary school, and I have nothing. Jillian
says four words and she gets a smile. Jillian moved here from
New York last fall semester and we sort of adopted her. I'm
starting to think maybe it's the other way around.

Jillian leans forward. "You will not believe what I saw
today."

"What?" I ask. I push the last of my cinnamon roll into my
mouth and try to wipe the stickiness off my fingers.

"Take a look for yourself," Jillian says, nodding toward

something behind me. Claire looks past me, a half smile forming on her face. I have to turn all the way around in my seat. What I see makes my heart beat too fast. Hillary King is standing with her back against one of the pillars. She is talking to her friend Katie, which in itself isn't weird. But she's doing it with her arms draped around some guy. And while I don't really care who the guy is, I do care a whole lot about who the guy isn't.

"Wild, huh?" Jillian asks. Claire is looking at me with her eyebrows raised. Luckily the bell for second period rings. Jillian is the first to break off, following some guy with a soccer ball under his arm down the main hall. I say good-bye to Claire at the stairs toward the art wing, giving her a little hug and a fresh stack of napkins I scored from the caff. I have to keep telling myself to calm down as I make my way toward trig. I mean, who Hillary King is or isn't currently dating should have no effect on me at all, but it does. Because if the scene in the caff is any indication, who she's not dating anymore is Ben Donovan.

chapter **four**

At Montrose, ninety-eight percent of the student body looks like they just stepped out of an Abercrombie & Fitch ad or just got kicked off *Top Model*. But even though breathtaking is pretty much the norm around here, Ben Donovan still parts the students in the hallways like he's Moses and they're the Red Sea. I mean, I've only spoken to Ben Donovan once and that was to stutter hello when he nodded at me on the pool deck. Pretty much every girl in school has probably daydreamed about Ben Donovan at one time or another. And the weird thing is even the teachers refer to him that way—Ben Donovan. Never just Ben. It's always first and last name. Ben Donovan, like even his name has to be set apart from the rest of us.

And if I had to say exactly why I've been crushing on Ben Donovan since I was in seventh grade, I probably couldn't. I mean, it just sort of happened. But it's not like anything will ever come of it. Ben Donovan is what Jillian calls "my ideal." She says we all need someone in our life who is completely impossible. It keeps us hoping. I'm not sure I believe that, but it's as good an explanation as any for the way my heart starts beating too fast whenever I see him.

I write his name across the top of my paper in fourth period, considering it. Mr. Reyes is blah-blahing about some poet named Rumi. I'm trying to figure out more sayings for my Consternation Hearts when my cell buzzes. And when I say buzzes, I mean it actually sounds like bees are inside of it, letting me know that Charlie has gotten to my phone. Weird ring tones are his specialty. We're not supposed to have phones in class, but everyone does. I slip my phone out of my pocket and hold it under my desk, so Mr. Reyes can't see. It's my mother. She's recently discovered texting, which means she can tell me things as she thinks of them, instead of having to wait for the rare moments when we're both free.

Working Late. Can u pick up L and D? M.

I think about the rising mountain of homework that is threatening to bury me. I start to text her back, asking if she can call Mrs. Bateman, but before I can finish, Mr. Reyes is standing beside me, his hand outstretched. Everyone in class watches me as I hand off my phone. The bell rings for lunch and I gather my books together. Mr. Reyes doesn't say anything as I walk past his desk. He just holds up my phone, along with a pink slip of paper. A detention. Hurray. This day just keeps getting better and better.

"Where do you want to eat?" Claire asks when I meet her at my locker. She seems better—a little less liquid.

"I'll be in The Pit," I say, holding up the pink slip. We can serve detention morning, noon, or after school. Since I'll be spending my afternoon with Lucy and Dom, I have to spend lunch in detention.

"Ouch," Claire says. "Sorry."

I shrug and try to be cavalier about it. "No big. Maybe I'll finally get caught up on my homework."

She nods. "I'll grab you something from the caff," she says. "Sushi?"

"Burger," I say.

"Your mother would be shocked." She smiles the tiniest bit when she says it. My mother is a well-known health nut.

Thinking less of my mother and more of my last three "meals"—peanut butter, bacon, and a cinnamon roll—I amend my order. "Veggie burger and carrot sticks."

"Enjoy The Pit."

I snort. Not one of my more ladylike characteristics. "Not likely," I say.

Claire smiles a little before heading toward the cafeteria,

which is a relief. At least little bits of Claire are still poking through. I start heading toward The Pit, a quaint nickname for the shop room where they have detention. Nothing like a little sawdust and the smell of motor oil to make you hungry. My phone buzzes again. I take a look before heading down the steps to the basement.

Thanks, P. Love M. I roll my eyes. She didn't even wait for my answer. She just assumed that I don't have anything else going on. And the sad thing is, other than homework, she's actually right.

I step into the land of cars and power tools and walk over to a stool near the back. I've only been here once before and that was because I refused to dissect a cat in biology. Ms. Heimer wanted me to spend the whole week in here, but one call from my mom and all I had to do was one day. I wipe at the decade of grime on the table with a rag that's been left there. I give up when I notice all I'm doing is moving the dirt around. I sit and drop my bag on the table in front of me. Mr. Bell, the shop teacher, is supposed to sit with us during detention, but all he does is take roll and give us a couple gruff sentences about hanging us up by our ankles if we mess around. Then he heads into his office and shuts the door. About three seconds later we hear the opening chords of a Zeppelin song.

I slide my Brit lit book out of my bag, trying to ignore the grunting from the other side of the room. Today's distraction seems to revolve around lifting something very big and very greasy. It's better than last semester, when they had a chew-spitting contest. I still feel vaguely ill when I smell anything wintergreen-scented.

The Pit is populated half by people in detention and half by students I've never seen anywhere else except here. Pitters don't look the same as the rest of the students. To be totally honest, I sort of admire Pitters. Even if they're gross, at least you know they're real.

There is a burst of yelling from the other side of the room as the Neanderthal Games really get going. I look over at Mr. Bell's office door, expecting it to fly open at any minute, but his only response is to crank up the squealing guitar solo. I sigh and try to find my place in my lit book. Mr. Reyes, ever the romantic, has assigned us Valentine's Day–related words for our homework. Just another reminder of how inescapable the holiday is. We're supposed to be prepping for the PSAT, and since Mr. Reyes is a self-proclaimed "logomaniac" (word lover), we just keep getting lists and lists of vocabulary. I've complained about him so much that my Christmas gift from Charlie was a calendar for my desk at home. It's called 365 Obscure Words. So far I've learned that mundungus is something that smells really bad and that mytacism is the incorrect use of the letter *m*. Useful stuff.

I look around The Pit and decide that this is the epicenter of mundungus-ocity. It's weird though. While The Pit is full-on nasty, the cars in here are pretty nice. From where I'm sitting, I can see one Mercedes, one BMW, one Lexus, and half a Hummer. In all truth, Montrose Academy is about as fancy as you can get.

"Look, the princess is back." A hand, almost as big as a page in my English book, plants itself on the table next to me. He's so close I can feel his breath on the side of my face. Wintergreen. I just keep working on my vocabulary, remembering another word from my calendar. Ablutophobia. A pathological fear of washing or bathing. "Hey, princess." I don't look up. Meat Hand pulls my book away from me, snaps it closed, and slides it across the table to another set of hands. Smaller, but equally grungy. I finally look up.

"Hey, Barry," I say. Like most everyone else at Montrose Academy, I've known Barry since we were in elementary school.

"The name's Booger," he says.

"And you prefer that to Barry?" I ask. He sneers at me, or at least he tries to. He needs to work on it, though, because it just looks like he's about to sneeze. "Can I have my book back?" I ask, reaching my hand across the table to where his sidekick is still holding it.

"What are you going to give me for it?" He attempts another sneer, but this one makes him look like he's in pain. I sigh.

"Gum?" I ask. It's the only thing I have in my bag besides books.

"How about a kiss, beautiful?" It's my turn to give a pained look. I'm not about to have my first kiss in The Pit with a guy named Booger. I try to think of something clever to say, something that will get my book back. Something that won't hurt Booger's pride and send my book into the nearest trash can. My chem book still smells minty-nasty from the chew glopped on it the last time I was in here.

"Leave her alone." The voice comes from the other side of one of the gutted cars they have scattered around the enormous room. Nearly everyone has been watching The Booger and Piper Show, mostly because there's nothing else to do. Now everyone, including me, turns to look at the guy coming around the back of the car.

"Why should I?" Booger asks, but his voice is definitely different. Less Booger. More Barry.

"Because you're not a total jerk." The guy coming around the car is definitely not like these other guys. In fact, I'm not sure he's even real. Because unless I'm starting to hallucinate from the fumes, the guy coming around the back of the car is Ben. Period. Donovan. Period.

"Jerk?" Booger begins. He looks like he's trying to figure out if this is worth the trouble. Apparently he decides it's not. "We're just messing around." He looks at me for confirmation, but I don't oblige. He reaches for my book. "Here," he says, pushing it hard enough to send it off the table and onto the floor.

"Thanks," I say. I start to say Barry, but decide to just go along. "Booger." He shrugs and heads back to the other side of the room, where they are starting up another game, this one involving a couple of long rubber tubes and a tire. I bend and retrieve my book, noting that there is now a big splotch of grease on the front. I gather my courage to say thank you to Ben Donovan, but he's gone already back around to the other side of the car. I get up and walk across the shop, careful of the grease smears along the way. I'm not really sure why it suddenly matters—my boots are designed to keep out just about anything.

When I circle the car, only the lower half of Ben Donovan is visible. His upper half is hidden under the car. "Thanks," I say to his feet. There's a clanging noise in response.

"Dang it." He rolls out from under the car. He stops when he sees me standing there.

"What?" he asks.

"I just wanted to—" For a moment I can't remember what it is I wanted to do. I just stand there looking at him. He frowns at me, then rolls to one side to grab another wrench out of the toolbox.

"Yes?" he says.

"I just wanted to say thank you." He stares at me. "So, um, thanks." He nods and looks around again, clearly still wondering what I'm doing here. I watch him for one more awkward moment before turning to walk back to my table and more irrelevant words.

"Hey, Piper," he says from behind me. I turn to find him staring at me with a half smile on his face. "Nice boots."

♥ **love?** maybe.

I feel my face get red. "Thanks," I say, because I have no idea what his half smile means. But it's definitely still there, and just as I'm about to ask him what he wants, he shakes his head and slides back under the car. I stare until all I can see are the bottom of his coveralls and his shoes. I try to focus on my English homework, but all I can think is that Ben. Period. Donovan. Period. actually knows my name.

Jillian is giving me "the look" again as I eat my lunch. Normally I have better manners, but I am starving and have only three minutes to shove food into my mouth before assembly. She's eyeing me like I'm one of those nature shows where you just know the cute little bunny is about to get it, but you can't stop watching.

"So, The Plan—" she finally says. Claire nods, looking past her to where a group of upperclassmen is climbing the steps from the caff and heading into the auditorium.

"Plan?" I ask around my last bite of veggie burger. I live for teasing Jillian.

Jillian sighs. "The Valentine's Day Plan. We now need to find *three* yummy guys."

I glance over at Claire, but she's not paying attention. She's still watching the stairs. Still looking for Stuart. "How about instead we find cupid and beat the stuffing out of him," I say. "Or we could all wear black. You know, in protest."

"Why are you so anti-Valentine's Day?" Jillian asks.

"Don't," Claire says.

"Don't what?" Jillian asks.

Claire looks over at me. "Too late."

I take a deep breath. "Valentine's Day is just a capitalist scam, designed to make people currently in a relationship spend unnecessary money in a fruitless attempt to ensure undying love and devotion. For those of us not in a relationship, Valentine's Day is simply added pressure to identify ourselves within the context of a romantic relationship, whipping us into a frenzy that only the presence of our soul mates can relieve."

Jillian rolls her eyes at me; Claire just shrugs. "I tried to warn you," she says. A group of rugby players mounts the stairs. Stuart is in the middle of the group as if he's hiding in their midst. He barely makes eye contact with Claire as he walks by.

"See?" I say to Jillian. "Why should we celebrate a day that is devoted to heartbreak?"

"I refuse to admit defeat," Jillian says.

Out of the corner of my eye I spot Jeremy lurking across the hall, probably trying to work up the nerve to say hello to Jillian. I smile in his direction, but Jillian glares at me and shakes her head. This of course makes me smile even more.

"We should go in," Claire says finally. "Afternoon assembly is about to start."

"I'll meet you in there." I notice that my hands are sort of gross from the veggie burger and probably I'm sort of grungy in general from my time in The Pit. Unfortunately, the closest restroom isn't all that close. I have to actually go outside and over to the next building. Even more unfortunately, it's raining. By the time I end up back in the main building, I'm pretty damp. Somehow, the twist my mother put in my hair is still holding up. But rubber boots + water + tile floor = an unbelievable amount of noise all in the form of loud squeaks that make it sound like I'm trying to smuggle a bunch of small rodents into the assembly.

As if the day couldn't get worse, the assembly has already started and Father Birch is up at the front leading everyone in an opening prayer. Claire and Jillian are about three rows down from where I'm standing at the back and they've left a seat for me on the aisle. *I can do this.* I walk carefully, trying to make as little noise as possible. Once I hit the carpet, I think I'm home free. But wet boots can slip as easily on carpet as they can on tile. The heel of my left boot catches on the edge of the step and my foot slides out from under me. My arms start pinwheeling. My legs fly out at weird angles and I brace myself for impact. I probably would have ended up sprawled halfway down the stairs with the whole school staring at me if it weren't for a pair of strong hands that manage to catch me before I hit the ground.

"Careful." The voice is low and soft and his breath is warm on my neck. I stand up unsteadily and make my way down one more step to where Jillian and Claire are sitting staring at me.

"Holy sugar," Jillian whispers in light of the fact that we're in chapel. "That was Ben Donovan." I shrug and both she and Claire look at me for a moment before turning their attention back to the front, where Father Birch is winding up the prayer. My cheeks still feel like they're on fire. Okay, so maybe I'm not completely hardened to the concept of romance. Or maybe I'm still dizzy from eating too quickly, almost falling on my head, and Ben Donovan's warm breath on my neck.

chapter **five**

The time it takes to pick up one almost-six-year-old from kindergarten and one almost-five-year-old from preschool is only slightly shorter than the time it took modern man to put someone on the moon. After three return trips (the first to retrieve one mitten, the second because Lucy did have to go to the bathroom after all, and the third because Dom forgot that it was his week to take home Chi Chi the Chinchilla), we finally manage to make it down the sidewalk and to the bus stop. We stand shivering behind the windscreen, waiting for the bus that will take us to my mom's shop. It's walkable from the school on a good day, but that day isn't today. Today, the wind is biting at us, making it scary cold, especially since this is Georgia. Here, you can bake cookies in your car in the summer (yes, we've tried it), and you can sometimes wear flip-flops in the winter.

"Piper, I'm cold," Lucy says for the seventh time. I look down and her teeth are actually chattering. I give up my scarf, twisting it around her neck and tucking the ends into the collar of her coat. Dominic refuses to zip up his coat, claiming he isn't cold.

"I'm hot," he says. Dom would argue that the sky is actually pink with yellow polka dots if you let him. Finally the bus rounds the corner and heads our way. I dig our bus passes out of my coat pocket and shift the three backpacks I am shouldering to try and make them stop cutting into my neck. The doors open and several people spill out. I have to grab onto Dom's hood to keep him from knocking into everyone as they walk past. Once aboard, Dom and Lucy shoot all the way to their favorite spot at the back, leaving me to juggle the passes, the backpacks, and Chi Chi's cage.

"Only service animals are allowed on the bus," the driver says, pointing to a sign posted on the front. I think quickly. The last thing I want is to have to walk the dozen blocks into the wind, dragging Lucy and Dom along behind me.

"This animal is being trained to retrieve objects for people." The driver peers into the cage. "Small objects," I say. He looks at my face, which is already flushed. I can see he doesn't believe me. I mean, I wouldn't believe me.

"Go sit down," he says, waving his hand toward the back.

"Thank you," I say. I start making my way toward the back, where Lucy and Dom are on their knees looking out the windows. When I'm halfway up the aisle, the bus lurches forward, sending me and Chi Chi sprawling to the floor. I push myself back to standing and peer into the cage. Chi Chi looks mad but unhurt. I wish I could say the same for me. Now, in addition to the run that wouldn't quite stay shoved into my boot, my tights sport matching holes in the knees. I sigh and sink into the nearest seat. I set Chi Chi's cage on my lap. Unfortunately I figure out too late that the dampness that is slowly leaking onto my legs through the air vents in the cage is not from the water tube. When the smell hits me, I realize that the spill scared Chi Chi more than he let on. And for the record, chinchilla pee is one of the worst smells you can imagine.

My mother's shop is called Lilly's Flowers. It's by far the nicest florist in Atlanta, mostly because my mom is a flower freak. A floraphilic. I hold the door open for Dom and Lucy as they race into the shop. My mother raises her eyebrows at me when she sees me. Not a good sign. Dom and Lucy run into the back, looking for the snack my mother always has laid out for them. I follow, letting our backpacks fall to the floor near the big walk-in refrigerator. I set Chi Chi's cage on the floor. Once my mother finishes waiting on a woman wearing an enormous red hat that has purple feathers hanging off of it in every direction, she joins us.

"Look what the cat dragged in," she says, smiling slightly. My mother is infinitely amusing. She tilts her head at me when I don't smile back. "Hard day?" I nod and lean against the wall. I feel like I've run seven marathons. "Hungry?" she asks. I nod again. I'm beyond speech at the moment, something that seems to be disturbing her. I file that away for the future. Nothing like having a little ammunition at your disposal when your parent is driving you nuts. My mother goes into the walk-in and comes out with a couple of apples and a bag of Jan's granola. My mother seems jittery and keeps fiddling with her earrings. She's also wearing makeup. That can only mean one thing.

"What time is Beau coming by?" I ask.

"Four," she says. The clock over the desk reads ten after.

I look at Dom and Lucy who are using their straws to blow bubbles in their milk.

"You sure he's coming?" I ask softly. Beau is not exactly Mr. Dependable.

"He said for sure this week." I bite my apple in frustration. Even though he moved out of our house over a year ago and almost directly into another woman's apartment, Mom still gets taken in by his charm. Just another example of the suckiness of love. Mom's cell buzzes and she pulls it from her pocket. She flips it open.

"Beau?" I ask. She nods and reads the message. Apparently Beau has also realized the benefit of texting.

"He said he has some business to take care of," Mom says.

"This is the third week in a row he's bailed on them."

"He's just busy, Piper," Mom says.

"And you're not?" She takes off her glasses and rubs the

bridge of her nose. "You have to stand up to him," I say.

"You don't understand," she says. I frown at my apple. I *do* understand. I understand that he's just using her feelings for him to take advantage of her. "Can you take them home with you?" she asks. I nod, frowning. I had hoped to have a little peace at home, but obviously that's not going to happen. I don't say anything though. I know whatever I might say, I'll regret. I sigh and start pulling my coat on again.

Mom manages to get Lucy and Dom cleaned up and out the door in about a third of the time it would have taken me. "Thank you, Piper," my mother says, holding the door for us. I just nod, still not trusting myself to say anything.

Even though Dom and Lucy don't mention their dad once on the walk home, it must be on their minds, because neither of them says anything at all. If there is anything worse than their constant bickering, it's this. I'm sure there's something in the big sister handbook about helping my younger brother and sister deal with life's pitfalls better than I'm doing. I just don't know what to say other than what I told Charlie. Divorce stinks.

I've just settled onto the couch with my jar of peanut butter and a spoon when my cell buzzes. I look at the screen before answering. Claire.

"Hey," I say around a mouthful of peanut butter. I pray she's feeling a little better.

"He's been cheating on me for months."

Okay. Deep breath. "How do you know this?" I ask.

"Bonnie overheard Ellen talking to Tracy in the locker room after gym." There seem to be two more layers of names, but I can't keep up. Montrose has to be the center of the gossip universe. Really, the administration should make it one of our electives. "She overheard Kelly talking to Christi."

"Wait," I say. "Which Christi?" There are four.

"Christi Jacobs."

"Oh," I say.

"Anyway, Christi was telling Kelly about the present Stuart gave her for Christmas." Claire sniffs hard again. "Christmas!" *Ouch.*

"Jerk," I say, dutifully. I may not be that familiar with the big sister handbook, but I'm a little clearer on the best friend one.

"That's not the worst part," Claire says. "Do you know what he gave her?" I stay silent. I have no idea where this is going. "He gave her a locket." A fresh wave of sobs pours through the phone. I sigh and close my eyes. Stuart just sealed my nomination for world's worst boyfriend. Claire had been hinting around for months that she wanted this locket she had seen in Jump!, the secondhand store where we always shop. It even had a *C* engraved on it, which I guess is why it worked for Christi too.

"He's a moron, Claire," I say, taking a page from Jillian's

book. "You don't need him. We are going to find you someone better," I say.

"You mean it?" Claire asks.

"Yes," I say. And I realize I do because my heart rate stays normal and my hands stay non-sweaty. Of course, I was totally willing to bust out a lie if I needed to. White lies are in chapter two of the best friend handbook. They are to be used sparingly and only under extreme circumstances. I'm pretty sure finding out your boyfriend of more than a year is a total jerk qualifies.

"Listen," I say. "Spend Friday night at my house." I really should ask my mom first before I invite friends to stay over, but I think I can play the jilted love sympathy card with her. "I'll call Jillian right now." Claire offers a watery thank you before hanging up. I leave a message on Jillian's cell, telling her about our planning meeting. I hang up just before I hear the sound of laughing followed by a big thud from upstairs. *So much for dinner,* I think, screwing the top back on the jar of peanut butter.

"How were they?" Mom asks, poking her head into my room.

"Good," I say. And it's the truth. For Dom and Lucy, they weren't terrible. I was able to clean most of the toothpaste out of their hair before I got them back into bed. Anything I missed will just give them that minty, freshly brushed scent.

"How are *you?*" she asks.

"I'm good," I say. My mother frowns and tilts her head at me. "Really." If I can just squeeze another half hour out, I'm pretty sure I can finish my paper, the one I begged an extension for.

"Don't stay up too late," my mother says, pulling my door shut behind her.

I sigh and rub my eyes. Literary criticism is so confusing. It seems like everything is symbolic. Nothing is just what it is. How am I supposed to know that a gray scarf is supposed to symbolize unrequited love? I manage to pull together something that should earn me at least a B, then take out our next novel, *Emma*. It seems that even my Brit lit teacher is conspiring against me in matters of the heart. I can only make it through a dozen pages before I have to admit that I'm just too tired.

I put down the novel and slide under my quilt. I think about one of the ten random questions that Dom asked me earlier. He wanted to know if I thought the sun got lonely. I told him I hadn't really thought about it, but that I imagine he did. It was the wrong answer. Dom got pretty quiet for the rest of the night. I turn off the light beside my bed, wondering if I should have told him something else. Something a little more upbeat. But, when I think about it, I'm sure the sun does get sad sometimes. He just sits up there, shining on everyone and keeping everyone rotating the way they're supposed to. But what about him? I wonder if sometimes he just looks around and says "Hey! What about me? Who's keeping the lights on for me? Who's making sure I'm not going to fall out of the sky?" I shake my head. Too much literary symbolism.

It's not until I'm almost asleep that I remember my promise to Claire. I try to come up with a plan—anything— but I've got nothing. I'm praying that Jillian has at least some idea of how to find Claire a boyfriend. I'm praying just as hard that she won't try to snag someone for me in the process. If there is one wish I have for Valentine's Day *and* my birthday, it's this: I'd like a little peace and quiet. A little fun maybe, and no drama.

chapter six

I'm doing the dishes in the bathroom sink when the door-bell rings. I'm hoping it's the plumber, but I'm pretty sure I know who it is.

"I'll get it," Dom hollers.

"Hold it," I yell, wiping my hands on the dish towel I have slung over my shoulder. Dom waits at the door, hopping from one foot to the other. Lucy is sitting on the sofa, her pink suit-case at her feet. I'm not sure what's worse, Dom's enthusiasm about seeing his father for the first time in a month or Lucy's sadness. I take a deep breath and open the door.

"Hi, sweetheart," Beau says, leaning forward and kissing my cheek. He reaches down and tussles Dom's hair. I step back to let him in. "It's so good to see y'all," he drawls. I hear my mother's footsteps above us. "Hey, Lucy. Don't you have a hug for your daddy?" Lucy stands up and walks over to him, giving him a stiff hug around the legs. "Hold it," Beau says as she starts to walk away. He reaches behind her ear and pulls out a necklace of pink beads and hands it to her. The necklace earns him a real hug and a smile.

"Now me!" Dom says, jumping up and down in front of him. Beau does the same trick with Dom. He opens his hand to reveal a new Matchbox car. Even though I've seen the trick about a million times, I still never see him palming anything.

"How about you, darlin'?" he says to me. I just shake my head. When I first met Beau, I begged him to marry my mother so he would be my father. Now I'm too old to be taken in by his charms. Hearing my mother coming down the stairs, I amend that thought. Maybe I'm just too cynical. "Hey, beautiful," Beau says when my mother appears. He walks over and kisses her cheek. She stiffens slightly, but she also blushes. I wonder where Stacy, his girlfriend, is.

"It's good to see you, Beau," my mother says. Beau offers her his best smile and I see her blush again.

"Whoops," he says, looking at his watch. "We've gotta skedaddle if we're going to make the movie." Dom and Lucy both start jumping up and down when he says that. "You sure you don't want to join us?" he asks me. I just shake my head. There was a time when I was younger that I would wait for Beau to get home just like Dom does, but not anymore. Beau Paisley is charming and handsome, but he's also unreliable and selfish.

My mother heads upstairs after saying good-bye to Dom

and Lucy. I watch them through the kitchen window as they make their way toward Beau's enormous truck parked in front of the house. The overhead light goes on as he opens the door, illuminating the inside of the truck. Perched in the passenger seat is Beau's girlfriend, Stacy. After Beau gets the kids settled in the back, he climbs in himself. The overhead light in the truck doesn't quite go out before he leans across and kisses her. Ugh. I didn't need to see that. There are soft footsteps above me. Someone else saw that too, and she *really* didn't need to see that. Or maybe she did. Maybe that will finally make my mother get it.

Claire and Jillian arrive within minutes of each other. We scrounge in the kitchen for snacks.

"Wasabi peas?" Jillian asks, shaking a plastic container of tiny green marbles. She goes back into the pantry and comes out with a bag of textured vegetable protein in one hand and a box of steel-cut oats in the other.

"My mom's a little bit of a health nut," I say.

"A little?" Jillian asks. "Your pantry looks like a mini Whole Foods. Don't you have any junk food?" I start to shake my head, but then I remember the chocolate. I have to climb onto one of the bar stools to reach it. I pull down a couple of long, flat boxes. "That's what I'm talking about," Jillian says. She grabs the box and pulls it open. The chocolates inside are all a little off. Most are misshapen or maybe have a hole in them.

"They're chocolate irregulars," I say. Jillian picks one up and sniffs it. "They taste the same. They just look funny." I tossed the rest of the Kalamata Caramel that Jan gave me. I just couldn't get over the olive and chocolate hurdle. Jan told me he's already sold out of them. Just one more reason why he's the confectionary genius and not me.

Jillian bites into one of the chocolates. "Oh man, I would weigh a thousand pounds if I worked there." She holds the box out. Claire takes one, but I shake my head.

"You'd get sick of it," I say. "I don't really like candy all that much." Jillian frowns at me. "After a million Saturdays being around chocolates, you'd swear off the stuff too."

"I doubt it," Jillian says, popping another into her mouth. She puts the top back on the box. "How did you start working there anyway?"

"When my mom and Beau were splitting up, it was someplace to go. Someplace quiet," I say, remembering the tears and the furious whispered arguments. Jillian nods like she understands. It makes me realize I know almost nothing about her family. It's like she's so out there, she's hidden.

"Piper's just being modest," Claire says. "When Jan first hired her to 'help him get organized'"—she makes air quotes as she says it—"Piper kept finding money everywhere." Jillian looks at me.

"It's true," I say. "There was seven hundred dollars stuffed in a plastic tub in the refrigerator and almost two thousand shoved in a file in one of the desk drawers." Jillian smiles at this. "I didn't have to do much. Start a filing system, set him up with electronic fund transfers for his vendors—" Jillian is staring at me. "It wasn't that big of a deal."

"Uh-huh," she says before popping another chocolate in her mouth.

"No, really. Jan's the genius," I say. "I'm just good at details."

"Don't listen to her," Claire says to Jillian. "Last year there was this whole write-up in the paper about Jan's. And the photo on the Food page was of Piper's taffy." I shrug, trying to play it off. The truth is I prefer being the behind-the-scenes person.

"Pretty cool, Piper," Jillian says. She lifts the top off the box and pops another chocolate into her mouth, looking a little sheepish.

"Have as many as you want. There are three more boxes up there," I say, pointing to the cabinet over the fridge. My mom always wanted me to bring them home. It kind of makes me sad. The only person who really ate them was Beau. Now I just hand them over to Charlie when he comes over.

Jillian swallows her chocolate and grabs her notebook. "Let's get down to business." She looks at me. "Knowing that you are so good at organization makes this all sort of weird, but I think we need to make a plan."

"I already have my plan," I say. "A large Vegetarian's Delight from Artie's and a stack of sci-fi movies and I'm all set."

"Pizza and spaceman movies?" Jillian asks. "That's your big plan? What about you?" she asks, elbowing Claire. "Do you really want to spend Valentine's Day on the couch?"

"No," Claire says. I raise my eyebrows at her. Claire looks over at me. "Please, Piper."

I take a deep breath. This is what best friends are for, I tell myself. "Fine," I say. "What do you want me to do?" Claire gives me a grateful smile.

Jillian smiles at me and puts the notebook on the counter, flipping pages until she finds one with a grid drawn on it. "We have less than two weeks until V-Day. It's important we are all committed to this. No matter what."

"No matter what?" I ask. "That seems a little intense. I mean, it's just a holiday."

"It's not just a holiday. It's love," Jillian says.

"Love?" I ask. I start to shake my head. I did not sign up for love, but the hopeful look on Claire's face makes me pause. "Okay." I sigh. "What's the plan?"

"The first step is finding two guys you want to target."

"Why two?" I ask. "I thought the plan was to find love."

"You always have to have a fall-back plan," Jillian says.

"A plan B," Claire says.

Jillian nods while I concentrate on not rolling my eyes. "Claire, you first."

Claire looks out the window for a moment and then back at us. "Stuart, obviously." Jillian writes his name in her notebook. "Then, I don't know."

"You need a backup," Jillian says.

"Alex Muñoz," she finally says.

Jillian stares at her. "Alex Muñoz?"

"You said I needed a backup and he's nice."

Jillian shrugs. "It's your heart." She looks at me. "Now you."

I feel my cheeks get red. "I don't think—"

"Ben Donovan," Claire says. I give her a dirty look, but Jillian just nods and writes him in her notebook then looks back up at me.

I think for a moment. "I don't know," I say. Jillian keeps looking at me. "The new exchange student. The one from England. I don't know his name."

"I *do* know his name," Jillian says. Of course she does. "Andrew Spence. He's sort of nerdy," she says.

"There's nothing wrong with nerdy," I say, feeling a little defensive. I mean, I'm pretty sure I'm a little nerdy.

Jillian puts her hand up. "I love a good nerd as much as the next girl, but just because I like nerds doesn't mean I want to date one," she says. "Okay, Andrew Spence." She writes his name under Ben Donovan. "He's a good choice." She starts to turn the page.

"Hold it," I say, putting out my hand to keep her from flipping to the next page. "What about you?"

Jillian shrugs. "Sam Harbo and Brett Rosen." Both Claire and I stare at her. She just named two of the most popular guys at Montrose Academy. Both seniors. Both cute. Both with girlfriends. And both completely out of our league.

"Wow," I say. "Nothing like aiming high."

Jillian shrugs. "They are my ideal," she says. I start to ask her how *two* different people can be her ideal, but again, she keeps moving forward. "I made notes for each of you," she says. She tears two pages from her notebook and hands one to each of us. Piper is written at the top of mine, with a bulleted list below. Jillian takes another chocolate from the box, watching us. I read the first few.

Dye hair.

Wear better shoes.

Stop slouching.

I look up at her. "What is this?" I lean over and look at Claire's. She has her own list. I notice dye hair is number one on her list too.

"Phase One of The Plan," Jillian says.

"What's wrong with my hair?" Claire asks. I look at her and shrug. I mean, my hair could use some work for sure, but Claire's looks, well, like Claire.

"Don't think of it as how it's wrong, but how it can be right," Jillian says.

"Isn't that the same thing?" I ask.

"It's all in the perspective."

I scan the rest of my list. "So all we have to do is become completely different people?" Claire looks at me and I remember my promise. "Okay, so where do we start?"

"I am so glad you asked," Jillian says. She riffles in her bag again and pulls out three boxes of hair color. I relax a bit when I see it's only semipermanent. She pulls out a bunch of other items, most of which I recognize, but several of which bear a strong resemblance to the medieval torture devices pictured in my history textbook.

An hour later, the three of us are sitting in my room with towels wrapped around our freshly dyed hair and green goop on our faces. Claire is tackling bullet number seven on her list and painting her toenails. Jillian keeps talking about my room and how it looks like cupid threw up in here.

"For someone who hates Valentine's Day . . ." she begins, gesturing at the twinkling heart-shaped Christmas lights I have strung on the ceiling over my bed. I'm lying on my back on the floor, trying to decide if the burning on my face is good burning or bad burning.

"Take a look at this," Jillian says. I lean up on one elbow, struggling to lift my head under the weight of the wet towel. I brace myself for more ribbing about my décor, but she's holding up a thin book. She tosses it to me. The cover is blank. I open it and flip through it quickly.

"A magic book?" I ask. Jillian nods. Claire glances at me, but she doesn't say anything. She just keeps painting her toenails.

"Look at chapter four," Jillian says. I flip through the pages. The first two spells seem pretty lame. If you sprinkle an infusion of roses and coriander on your front porch, *true love will come calling*. Holding my place, I flip back to the beginning, looking for an author's name. There isn't one. The date of publication, though, is listed as 1872. Weird. The second spell claims that your love will never stray if you feed him or her raw garlic at least once a day. I smirk. Yeah, that's some good magic. I keep flipping pages. Nothing seems very magical. Most of it seems like common sense that at best *might* work. The last spell in the chapter makes me pause. *Love Potion*. I look over at Jillian, who is smiling at me. I read the spell. Unlike the other spells, there isn't much explanation with this one. Just a list of ingredients and a couple of sentences about harmonizing and steeping and infusing.

I toss the book back on the bed and Jillian picks it up. "So what do you think?" she asks me. "Do you think this actually works?"

"No."

Jillian barely pauses. "But if it did," she says.

"If it did, don't you think someone else would have figured it out by now?" I ask.

"Maybe," Jillian says, but then she's quiet. A silent Jillian is even more disturbing than a chattering one. Before she can start up again, there is a huge *thunk* on the roof above us. Jillian screams, dropping the spell book behind the bed.

"It's just Charlie," I say. I go to the window and lean out. "Come to the front," I say. Charlie leans down over the edge of the roof.

"What's on your face?" he asks. I had forgotten the green stuff on my skin. I feel my cheeks heat up.

"Hush. Be nice or no chocolate for you." He keeps smirking at me. "Come to the front," I repeat. He waves and I hear his footsteps retreat across my roof and back to his own. I pull my head back in and close the window. Jillian is looking at me from the bed. Claire is trying to wipe the nail polish from the top of her foot where it landed when Jillian screamed.

"Who was that?" Jillian asks.

"Just Charlie," I say. "He's coming over."

"A guy is coming here?" Jillian asks. I nod. Jillian launches from the bed. "I've got to get cleaned up."

Charlie reeks of chlorine, which at the moment is probably the least offensive thing about him. In the few minutes he has been here, he's eaten half a loaf of bread, an apple, all six of the Peanuttiest truffles I brought him, and most of a block of cheddar. He eats it all standing up, letting the crumbs fall into the kitchen sink. My mother is always after Charlie to eat, telling him he's too skinny. I'm pretty sure he doesn't need the encouragement. Charlie reaches into the cabinet over the fridge and pulls out one of the boxes of candy.

He drops two chocolates in his mouth and is silent for a moment. "Mocha and . . ." He pauses and tilts his head to one side. "Strawberry." He grabs two more. "So, I told coach he can either let me anchor or he can take me off the

IM roster," he says. I nod. Jillian and Claire just look at him. Claire seems slightly horrified by him like she always is, but from the way Jillian is looking at him, you'd think Charlie was wearing wings and a halo instead of a pair of ripped sweatpants and an old thermal shirt.

"What did your coach say?" I ask. I still have a few days before my spring practices start up. Unlike Charlie, I am not a natural swimmer. I have to work really hard just to stay on the team.

"He said I could anchor if I swim the thousand." He grimaces at me, but I can't tell if it's from the swimming or from the pickle he's inhaling.

"Ouch," I say.

Charlie nods. "Hey, you know what would be even better than candy?" He nods at the half-eaten box of chocolates. "Freshly baked cookies."

"Dream on," I say, shaking my head.

"We could make them," Jillian says. She looks at me with big eyes and nods slightly.

I squint at her. "I guess," I say and shrug. I start pulling ingredients out of the refrigerator and the pantry.

"I like oatmeal raisin," Charlie says. He leans against the counter and watches me, smirking.

"You'll eat what I make and like it," I say.

"So, Pipe, how many days until your birthday?"

"Sixteen?" I crack an egg against the counter. "Seventeen?"

"Who are you?" Charlie asks. He turns toward Claire and

Jillian. "What have you done with Piper?" I throw the bits of eggshell in his direction and he ducks, laughing. "This from the girl who used to start the countdown weeks out. She used to tell everyone how many more shopping days until her birthday."

"That was a long time ago," I say, stirring the mass of sugar, butter, and eggs in the bowl.

Claire laughs from where she is sitting at the counter. "Piper, you were still doing that in middle school."

"That was before," I say.

"What? Before you got cynical?" Charlie asks.

"I'm not cynical," I say.

"Well, you're not *not* cynical," Charlie says.

I frown into the bowl as I stir. It's more like I just learned not to get my hopes up about anything, but I guess now that I think about it, that sounds pretty cynical.

Jillian perches on one of the bar stools pulled up to the counter and watches. Even though she's the one who wanted to make cookies, it's obvious I'm the one who is actually going to do the work. She starts firing all kinds of questions at Charlie. Where does he go to school? What movies does he like? What music does he listen to? He does his best to keep up, but she's relentless.

"Where's Stuart?" Charlie asks when Jillian pauses. I make a slicing motion at my throat, but Charlie just looks at me. I shake my head and start spooning mounds of dough on the cookie sheet.

"I don't know," Claire says. Her voice cracks a little in the middle, but her face remains placid. Luckily Charlie gets the point and doesn't ask anything else. Not that he has a chance to. Jillian starts attacking him with questions again.

Claire keeps taking her phone out of her pocket every three seconds to look at it. I told her to block Stuart's calls, but she won't. She said he might need her. I think he lost the right to need her when he dumped her. I also think that if she blocks his calls, she can pretend that he called, but she just couldn't get them. I know it's a silly game, but it works with me. I blocked my dad's calls on my cell a long time ago. Not that he's calling, but at least I can pretend that he still thinks about me.

I slide the pan of cookies in the oven and twist the tomato-shaped timer to twelve minutes. I lean against the counter and watch Jillian flirting with Charlie. He seems mostly oblivious to her, more interested in sneaking fingerfuls of dough out of the mixing bowl than listening to her talk about where she spent her winter break. Jillian is about to launch into a description of the boat she and her family stayed on when Charlie stretches. She stops talking and just watches. I look over at him, but honestly I can't see what she's getting so bunched up over. He's just Charlie.

The timer rings and I take the cookies out. The four of us stand around and eat them hot off the pan. I notice that Jillian only takes one. I wonder if it's because she already filled herself up with candy or if she's trying to be dainty in front of Charlie. I hate it when girls do that. It's not like it's some big secret that we eat. Besides, I don't think guys care about half the stuff girls think they do. As far as I can tell, guys care about sports and food and sleeping. And maybe girls. But as Dom says, only if they're not too yucky.

"Does your girlfriend come watch you at your meets?" Jillian asks. *Smooth,* I think.

"No," Charlie says, scooping up another hot cookie. I look at him. Last I knew he was dating Julie Reynolds.

"No as in she doesn't or no as in you don't have one?" Jillian asks. I have to hand it to her. She's nothing if not direct.

"Don't have one," Charlie says. This seems to cheer Jillian considerably. She smiles as she takes another bite of her one cookie.

"Listen, I have to take off," Charlie says. He pushes the rest of cookie number five into his mouth. "Early practice." He scoops up two more cookies and heads toward the door. "Thanks for the cookies, Pipe." He opens the door. Miss Kitty bolts between his legs and bounds up the stairs. He doesn't say anything about the purple Sharpie swirls that still decorate her fur. "Nice meeting you," he says to Jillian. He looks over at Claire, who is sliding her phone out of her pocket again. "Hey," Charlie says. She looks up. "His loss." She gives him a smile. I smile at him too. Charlie can be incredibly thick sometimes, but every once in a while he does something that reminds me of why we're friends. He has barely closed the door behind him when Jillian turns to me.

"Why didn't you tell me?" she asks.

"Tell you what?" I slide the sheet pan into the sink.

"Tell me your next door neighbor is such a hottie!"

"Did you just use the word hottie?" I ask, shaking my head at her. I have to fight the impulse to roll my eyes. Sometimes she talks like she's the star of her own reality show. I look over at Claire, hoping she's going to field this one, but she's staring at her phone again. I pull out some plastic wrap to cover the rest of the cookie dough. Maybe I'll surprise Dom and Lucy with homemade cookies when they get home from Beau's.

"Have you and Charlie ever gone out?" Jillian asks.

"Ew," I say. "No."

"Why ew?" Jillian asks. "He's dee-lish."

"Double ew," I say. "Charlie is just . . ." I pause. "He's just Charlie," I say. "We've known each other forever." I slide the bowl of dough into the fridge. "Besides, I'm not his type."

"What is his type?" Jillian asks with considerable intensity.

"I don't know," I say. "I just know it's not me. He's seen me at my worst. Trust me." Jillian's still looking at me. "He's seen me with poison ivy on my eyelids, blue hair, and dressed up as a pineapple." I hold up my hand. "I can promise you Charlie Wishman has no romantic designs on me whatsoever."

"Well, he is droolable," Jillian says. "Seriously."

I roll my eyes and look to Claire for backup. She is looking at Jillian too, and I wonder if she's thinking the same thing

I am. *Mental.* We clean up the kitchen. By we, I mean me. Jillian watches, peppering me with questions about Charlie every seven seconds. Claire alternates between staring off into space and checking her phone. As I push the eggshells down the disposal, I consider chucking Claire's phone in there as well. She has to stop.

When we head upstairs, I pause in front of my mother's door. She's quiet and I wonder if she's fallen asleep. We decide to postpone any more of Jillian's list until the weekend. I am just about to fall asleep in the nest I constructed out of a couple of camp blankets and a pillow from Dom's bed when Jillian leans over the side of the bed to look at me.

"I think we should try the potion," she says.

"The love potion?" I ask. She nods. *Definitely mental.* "Please tell me you're joking."

"We should do this for Claire," Jillian says. I look over at Claire, but she's sound asleep. I think about the look on her face when she saw Stuart on the stairs and how she keeps checking and rechecking her phone.

"Okay," I say. I sigh and close my eyes. "For Claire,"

"It says for best results, they have to ingest it." I try to imagine handing Ben Donovan a vial of pink goo and asking him to drink it.

"Not going to happen," I say.

"I have a plan."

"Tell me," I say, although I'm not one hundred percent sure I want to know.

"We need a kitchen and about twenty bucks." I think about the kitchen at Jan's.

"We?" I ask.

"Yes, we."

I sigh and roll onto my side. I'm sure any other girl on the planet would be all over Jillian's Love Makeover plan. But even if a tiny part of my heart bumps when I think of the way Ben Donovan keeps smiling at me whenever we pass in the hall, if it weren't for Claire, I'd bail on the whole idea. Then I look over at her, still holding her phone set on vibrate, and I know I'm in this. At least as long as she is.

chapter seven

Most Saturdays I help out in Jan's. It's easily my favorite place in all of Atlanta for many reasons. First, working at Jan's gets me out of watching Dom and Lucy and helping Mom at the flower shop. Second, Jan finally talked me into making candy last year, and although I grumble about it, I secretly really love it. Third, what Claire and I told Jillian is true. Jan is sort of eccentric and a terrible businessman. He's always giving out free stuff. If it weren't for my help with the books, half of me wonders if he wouldn't have already gone out of business. Helping Jan makes me feel like I'm actually making a difference, even if it's a small one. And fourth, Jan is about the best listener I know. He doesn't say that much, but when he does, he's all deep and mystical.

Jan and I are restocking the Valentine's Day corner. "I told Claire she just needs to forget Stuart." I straighten the sign advertising my Consternation Hearts, which go on sale Monday. "But she can't. It's like her whole world ended." I fill a glass vase with a dozen heart-shaped lollipops. "And Jillian," I say, standing up to look at Jan, who is stacking box after box of gummy hearts, "she is driving me nuts with The Plan." So far The Plan seems to consist of makeovers and a love potion, but I have a feeling there's a lot more to this than Jillian is letting on. I bend and plug in the twinkling pink and red lights around the window. I take my banana out from under the counter and peel it. I love bananas, but only if they are completely yellow. No brown and definitely no bruised parts. I take a few bites and study the candy case. There are a lot of empty plates that need to be filled.

"What about you?" Jan asks.

"What about me what?" I ask around my mouthful of banana.

"You talk a lot about what Claire and Jillian think about love. What about you?"

"Love? No thank you." I take my last bite of banana and toss the peel into the trash.

"I don't know," Jan says. He pauses so long I think he's finished, but then he takes a deep breath. "I think love is like candy."

"I don't like candy, either," I say. I pick up a rag and wipe off the menu board on the wall and start listing the new flavors.

He smiles at me and shakes his head. "I think anyone who

says they don't like candy just hasn't found the right flavor."

I roll my eyes at him. "Thank you, Master Yoda."

"See the wisdom of my words one day you will." I shake my head and add a sketch of a coconut kissing a pineapple beside Island Paradise. Jan plugs in the juke-box and punches a button. He starts singing along with some song about a guy trying to place a call to someone who broke his heart. He moves chairs, stools, and various other seats around as he sings. He has a little café set up in the middle of the store. For seats there's a saddle mounted on a sawhorse, one of those huge exercise balls glued to a platform, and a throne fit for a king—all for customers to sit on. He had a toilet seat for one day, but everyone was pretty grossed out by it.

I fix my ponytail, pulling my freshly-colored hair through my pink elastic. Honestly I can't tell the difference, but Jillian said it looks a thousand times better.

"You ready?" Jan asks, flipping the sign. I nod and climb down off the stool. From the moment Jan turns the lock on the front door, we're slammed. Everyone keeps asking about my Consternation Hearts. There was a write-up in the paper along with all the other Valentine's Day hoopla coming up. I had originally wanted to start selling them mid-January, but getting the packaging together so they look like the original conversation hearts was trickier than I thought.

The big seller of the day is one of Jan's inventions: For-tune Hearts. I'm pretty sure he works all year on the little sayings he has printed on the foil wrappers of the tiny choco-late hearts. He's been selling them since he started this shop and he sells out every year, usually way before Valentine's Day. People actually start calling in with orders for them right after Christmas.

Jeremy comes in mid-afternoon. He barely looks at me, but makes a beeline for Jan. He and Jan spend several moments deep in conversation. Then Jeremy leaves, still without making eye contact with me.

"What was that all about?" I ask Jan when he comes back around the counter. Either he ignores me or he just doesn't hear me because it's so noisy, but either way he doesn't answer.

Jillian and Claire arrive just as we're about to close up. They help mop the floor and wipe down tables while I fill napkin holders and replenish the jar of fortune hearts Jan keeps by the register.

When we are finally finished, Jan corners me in the kitchen. "Okay," he says, holding up his key ring. "Do not turn on the stove or lock yourselves in the walk-in." He starts to hand the key to me, but yanks it back at the last moment. "Do not set your heads on fire or cut off any digits or otherwise maim, injure, or damage yourselves."

"We promise," I say, putting my hand over my heart. Jan looks over at Claire and Jillian, who quickly do the same.

"I'm locking the door on the way out." He pulls his denim jacket off one of the pegs on the back wall. "I'll be back in two hours," he says. We begged him to let us have the kitchen to ourselves. We told him we wanted to try to create a new truffle (which is true) and that we wanted it to be a surprise. He pushes the back door open and steps out into the alley behind the shop. I start to pull the door closed, but he stops me. "Don't answer the door or the phone."

"You worry too much," I say. "We'll be fine." He lets the door shut and I hear him lock it from the outside. We can still get out, but no one without a key can get in. I gently push the door open to make sure he's gone. I watch him climb into his car. I shut the door and walk back into the kitchen. Claire and Jillian are already unpacking the back-pack that Jillian brought with her. A dozen baggies soon lit-ter the counter. I pick up the nearest, a bright gold one, and read the label: Tumeric. I scan the others: crystallized ginger, curry, cat's claw, fenugreek, burdock root, and several I can't even pronounce. Along with the bags, there are several plas-tic tubs: raw honey, acai extract, rose water. "Promise me we aren't going to poison anyone."

"I promise," Jillian says, putting her hand over her heart just like I did with Jan. Hopefully I was a little more convincing.

I pull two big bowls of the truffle base out of the refriger-ator. Jan left us some of both the vanilla base and the choco-late base. He was really excited when I told him I wanted to try and develop a new flavor of truffles. Of course, develop-ing the chocolates for Jan is just a cover. All we needed was private access to a kitchen. Somewhere away from the prying eyes of parents and the two munchkins who live at my house.

Jillian has the spell book on the counter in front of her. "There's not much in the way of directions here," she says. "I guess we just mix it all together?" She looks at Claire and me and we both shrug. She nods to herself like that settles it. Claire retrieves a big metal bowl from under the counter and we start adding all of the ingredients. A soft pattering sounds on the roof above us. Rain.

"How much?" I ask, holding a bag full of dried raspberry leaf.

Jillian shrugs. "All of it, I guess." Once we've dumped everything in, Claire mixes it all with a long metal spoon.

"It's potent," I say, catching a whiff of the mixture.

Claire sneezes. I notice her eyes are watering. "It smells like Pit Pot, the Indian restaurant my parents always take me to."

"Maybe we added too much curry," I say.

Jillian bends and sniffs the mixture. "It's perfect," she says. I want to ask her how she knows, seeing as this is the first time any of us has ever done this, but I just let it go. Her confidence seems to bolster Claire, making her smile. "We're supposed to let it *harmonize* for ten minutes," she says, reading from the spell book again.

"So, Pipe?" Claire says. "When are you going to show us?"

"Show you what?" I ask, smiling. Claire tosses a towel at

my head, making me duck. I was just waiting for them to ask. I walk over to the storage shelves and pull down a huge bin filled almost to the brim with candy. I set it on the counter and open it. Claire and Jillian come over immediately and peer over my shoulder.

"They're exactly like the real ones," Claire says, reaching into the bin and plucking a pink heart from the big mass. I nod. They came out amazing. I didn't actually manufacture all of the candy myself this time. I made the prototype and Jan found a confectionary company with the right equipment to churn them out way faster than we could have.

Jillian leans over and reads the heart Claire is holding. "Not Likely." She nods and leans over the bin, reading some of the others aloud. "Yuck, Go Away, U Stink." She looks over at me. "Harsh," she says.

I laugh and look into the bin. "These are pretty tame. You should have heard some of the ones—" I stop and look over at Claire. She gives me a small smile.

"Stuart had some harsh ones," she agrees. "Take Off, U'R Lame, Seriously?."

"They're cool, Piper," Jillian says, but her voice sounds unsure.

"What?" I ask.

Jillian looks at me for a long moment then just shakes her head. "They're cool. Just sort of—" She shakes her head again. "Nothing." I start to tell her to just say it, but she's already walking back toward where the mixture has apparently finished *harmonizing*.

"I think we have to do chocolate," she says, sniffing the mixture again. "Maybe it will hide some of the strong flavors." Whatever Jillian was going to say is gone now. We scoop some of the chocolate base into a small bowl, sprinkle it with a few spoonfuls of the mixture and stir. We each dip our fingers in and taste it.

"Not bad," Claire says. The rain intensifies, becoming an insistent thrumming on the roof above us.

"Okay," Jillian says. "Now the second part of the spell. Repeat after me—"

"Wait," Claire says. "What if Jan wants to use this?" She looks from me to Jillian. "I mean, what if he does and it works?"

I start to say something about the likelihood of the spell working being about the same as the likelihood of cupid flying out of my nose, but Jillian, sensing I'm about to say something sarcastic, elbows me.

"More love to go around, I guess," I say. Claire seems unconvinced. "What's the worst that could happen?" I ask. I realize I sound like the heroine of nearly every monster movie ever made. Right before the tomatoes turn from harmless salad additions to giant mutant man-eaters. Right before they figure out the green slime is really alien snot that has mind-controlling capability. I shake the thoughts from my head. This is real life, not Hollywood. Jillian and Claire are both staring at me. "It'll be fine," I say. Both of them seem way more caught up in this whole thing than I am. I think about Charlie calling me cynical.

"Okay then," Claire says. "What are we waiting for?" She reaches over and squeezes my hand.

"Repeat after me," Jillian says. I hope the fact that she's getting seriously impatient doesn't ruin the spell. I think about telling her that, but decide that impatient is better than ticked off, which is what she'll be if I interrupt her again. *"Elduanai Islandera pulatera. Let my love come to me."* Just as we finish, a huge crash sounds and all the lights in the kitchen blink out at once, pitching us into total darkness.

Jillian screams. Claire, who is standing closest to me, clutches my arm. My heart is thudding hard in my chest, but I'm the first to start laughing. Claire joins me and soon all three of us are laughing. "Do you think it was magic?" Jillian asks in the darkness.

"More like just a power outage," I say. I walk carefully over to the desk, hitting my hip once on the edge of the counter. I retrieve the flashlight that Jan keeps in the top drawer. I snap it on and point it toward where Claire and Jillian are standing. They squint against the light. There is a scrabbling at the back door.

"Don't answer it," Jillian says. I turn the beam of light on the door. There's more noise, then knocking. Suddenly all of the monster movies I have ever seen converge and I envision a huge lizard/tomato/zombie creature on the other side of the door. I walk toward the door on rubbery legs. Just as I reach it, there is more knocking, and then I hear my name.

"Don't," Claire says from behind me. I push the door open. The person standing there is just a shadow against the lights in the parking lot. Then the person speaks.

"I told you not to open the door," Jan says, walking in. He has his keys in his hand.

"But you knocked," I say. My voice comes out squeakier than normal. "Why didn't you just let yourself in? You have the key,"

"I couldn't see the lock in the dark." He props the door open with an empty crate to let a little light into the dark kitchen. "I heard screaming," he says. He must have been hanging out in his car this whole time. He really does worry too much. "Why are all the lights out?" he asks. He reaches for the light switch beside the door and toggles it once. Nothing. He walks over to the desk and reaches behind it where a small metal door is hidden. We hear a click, then the lights snap on. "You tripped a breaker somehow." I look over at Claire and Jillian, who both look a little sheepish. Although I have to admit, for a moment I got caught up in the whole idea of magic too.

"Hmm, something smells good," Jan says. He walks over to where our concoction is still steeping in its bowl. Jan slides a spoon from the drawer and dips it into our potion. He puts it in his mouth and tilts his head to the side. "Good," he says. He coughs once. "Spicy." He laughs. "I think we have a winner," Jan says. We help him mix a big batch of the new flavor and pour it into the molds. We slide the full trays into the refrigerator.

Jillian scoops what's left of our potion into a large glass jar, which Jan caps and slides into the refrigerator. He runs water into the bowl and adds a squirt of soap. "So, how's *The Plan* going?" Jan asks. Claire's cheeks go pink and my heart starts beating too fast. Only Jillian seems calm.

"Right on track," she says, smiling. Jan looks at me, one of his eyebrows raised. I look away, pretending to be intent on untying the strings of my apron.

"Hey," Jan says, turning off the water. "I almost forgot." He walks out the back door and comes back in carrying a big box. He puts it on the counter next to the bin of Consternation Hearts and uses a knife to slice open the tape. The three of us crowd around Jan and try to peer over his shoulders. Inside are hundreds of flattened pink boxes, each with a heart-shaped window covered in plastic on the front.

"Perfect!" Jillian says, pulling one out and folding it. She holds it up.

"It looks really good, Piper," Claire says.

"They do," I say. I didn't really think they'd look this good, this much like the real thing.

"Okay, now we just have to fill them all," Jan says. I take a deep breath and look at the thousands of pastel hearts jumbled together in the bin. That is going to be a huge job. A horn beeps out front.

"That's my mom," Jillian says.

"I'll come back tomorrow and fill boxes," I say.

"We'll help," Claire says. I look over at Jillian, who nods, although with slightly less enthusiasm than Claire.

"Okay then," Jan says, putting the top back on the bin of Consternation Hearts. "Until tomorrow." We gather our backpacks and coats and follow Jan through the darkened store to the front, where Jillian's mother's car is idling. "Thank you for the new flavor," Jan says, unlocking the front door and following us out onto the sidewalk. "It's going to be huge!" His exuberance makes us laugh. He waves at Jillian's mom as we get into the car. She waves back, smiling more than I think I've ever seen her smile. You can't *not* smile around Jan. All three of us push into the backseat, despite protestations from Jillian's mom that it makes her feel like our chauffeur. Just as I'm about to close the door, I hear Jan call my name. I peer out.

"What should we call the new flavor?" he asks. I don't even pause.

"Love Potion Number Nine," I say. Jan laughs.

"Perfect," he says. *If only he knew.* I wave again and pull the car door shut.

The three of us are so quiet that Jillian's mother tells us it's making her nervous. I wonder if Claire and Jillian are wondering the same things I am. What if the blackout wasn't an overloaded fuse as Jan suggested? What if it really was magic? What if our potion does work? I smirk at the ridiculousness of what I'm thinking. No way, I think. But then why does my heart do a little bump when I think of what might happen when I give Ben Donovan some of our chocolates? Thank goodness the backseat is so dark. At least no one can see me blushing.

chapter eight

It's after ten A.M. by the time I finally force myself out of bed. It's so rare the house is quiet enough to sleep past dawn that I decided to take advantage of it and not set my alarm. Usually by about six thirty either Dom or Lucy or both have been in here half a dozen times to see if I'm up yet. Since they're at Beau's for the whole weekend, it's quiet—almost too quiet. I pull on this hideous, old sweater I found at Jump! over my pajamas. The sleeves are so long I have to roll them several times to even see the tips of my fingers. I pull my hair into a sloppy bun on top of my head as I walk downstairs.

Mom is sitting at the counter sipping from a mug with her calendar spread in front of her. She glances up and smiles at me as I walk into the kitchen, but then looks right back at her calendar, making a notation off to one side with a pencil. It's no mystery where I get my organizational skills.

"How many?" I ask, pouring myself a mug from the cof-feepot.

"Well," she says, without looking up. "Plus the four orders I just took off the voice mail, it's two thousand one hundred and forty-eight flowers."

"Whoa," I say.

"Whoa indeed," she says. She frowns at her calendar. "It's going to be tight this year. I just don't have the cooler space I need."

"No luck with the expansion?"

She shakes her head. "They just won't budge. I mean, hon-estly. Jersey Mike's Subs doesn't need *another* dining room." She has been trying to get the sandwich shop next door to release their hold on the space between them, but so far they won't.

"It's not the greatest location anyway," I say.

"I know, but the thought of finding another location and then moving and . . ." She trails off, frowning at her calen-dar again. I take a sip of the coffee, grimacing at the taste. I forgot how strong my mother makes it. It seems like it just keeps getting stronger and stronger the longer we're in the busy season. By the time the June weddings finally end, I almost need a fork to drink it. My mother's cell rings. Just a normal ring, not the dog barking that Charlie just put on my phone to replace the bees. She puts the phone to her ear. "Hello?"

♥ **love?** maybe.

I open the fridge and peer in, trying to find something decent for breakfast. Something other than the acai juice my mother is currently hooked on. I push past a banana with too much brown and grab a quart of strawberries. I take them over to the sink and flip the faucet up to wash them. Nothing. I keep forgetting. The sink is *still* broken.

"Today?" my mother says into her phone. "Oh well, if that's the only—" I look over at her to see her looking at me. She glances back at her calendar and frowns again. "No, no. This afternoon will be fine." She clicks her phone closed. "That was a plumber."

"And—"

"And they're willing to come take a look at it, but it has to be today."

I'm not sure why she's frowning at that information. It's been nearly a week without water in the kitchen. We've been making do with the downstairs bathroom, but even with the lid closed, there's something disturbing about putting the dish drainer on top of the toilet. "But, that's good right?" I ask. She bites her lower lip. "Oh," I say. "Someone needs to be here to meet the plumber."

"Piper, I am so sorry," Mom says. "I know I have been asking so much of you. I mean, with Mrs. Bateman out sick and unable to babysit and with Valentine's Day right around the corner—"

I hold up my hand. "It's okay," I say. "I didn't have any plans." I feel my pulse start racing as I say it.

"Really?" she asks.

I nod, not trusting my voice to the lie. My palms get clammy and I can feel my cheeks start to get pink. "Well," I say, before any more symptoms hit, "nothing I can't change."

My mother gets up from where she is sitting and comes around the counter. "Thank you, Piper," she says. "I promise I'll make it up to you."

"I'll make a list," I say, smiling. She gives me a hug before closing her calendar and heading up the stairs. I dig out my cell phone and dial Jan's. I tuck the phone between my shoulder and my ear as I walk toward the bathroom with the container of strawberries in my hand. I'm trying to decide which is worse, eating unwashed strawberries or washing strawberries in the bathroom sink, when Jan's voice mail clicks on. I quickly run the berries under the water as I explain why I can't be there to fill boxes of Consternation Hearts.

After inhaling the last of the strawberries, I open the pantry door to put the empty plastic container in the re-cycling and find it already overflowing onto the floor. I take the whole box outside to dump it in our recycling can, but it too is overflowing. I peek over at the Wish-man's can just across the small strip of lawn between our houses. I decide in the interest of saving the planet that it's okay to dump our recycling in their bin. Besides, with only Charlie and his dad living in the house, how much could be in there?

The front door opens just as I'm shaking out the last can. Mr. Wishman steps out onto the porch.

"Morning, Mr. Wishman," I say.

He glances in my direction and offers me a weak smile. "Morning, Piper," he says. I start to thank him for letting me use up some of their recycling space, but he turns and heads back inside before I can.

Charlie's dad has always been a little eccentric. He's a great artist and a really nice person, but things like clean clothes, haircuts, and mealtimes seem to fall off his radar when he's painting. I'm guessing he must be in the middle of something huge.

The good news is that I've gotten almost all of my homework done. The bad news is that the plumber, who was supposed to show up "sometime after lunch," doesn't even make it to the front door until nearly four. The worst news is that it's already after five and all I can see is the bottom half of him still sticking out of the cabinet under the kitchen sink. He keeps complaining to me about the "old pipes" in this house, like it's my fault they are all corroding and breaking down. My mother's called half a dozen times from the shop, each time expressing her thanks more and more earnestly for staying here with him. My cell barks at me. I look over at the legs sticking out from under the sink and surmise that the bits of pipe scattered all around them mean it's still going to be a while.

"Hey, Jan," I say. I can hear "The Way You Look Tonight" through the phone.

"Just calling to let you know that as of tomorrow your Consternation Hearts are officially on sale."

"You finished?" I can't stop grinning. I couldn't figure out how I was going to get all those boxes filled and still actually attend school this week. "Thank you so much, Jan. You—"

"Whoa," he says. "Don't thank me. All I did was fold up a few boxes between customers. Your friends did all the work."

"Are they still there?" I ask.

"Nope," he says. "They just left. Something about *The Plan.*" I roll my eyes. No telling what Jillian has Claire doing now. Bleaching her teeth. Getting a facial. Balancing her chi. "I sent them out of here with a few of boxes of Love Potion Number Nine and a bag of Morning Madness Granola about ten minutes ago." *Here we go,* I think.

"How does everyone like the new flavor?" I ask.

"It's not officially on sale yet," Jan says. "Although Jeremy tried it when he came in early to help me open up. He said it was good."

I smirk at the thought of Jeremy trying the new flavor. He doesn't need any help in the falling in love department. "Jeremy is working there now?" I ask. Man, that guy is un- stoppable.

"Just here and there," Jan says, laughing. "Don't worry. Your job isn't in jeopardy."

Just then plumber guy starts griping again from under the sink, something about flanges and crimping. "I better go," I say.

"Drop by after school so you can see your new creation in all its glory," Jan says. "I have them right in the window along with a sign advertising the new truffle of the month."

"Thanks again, Jan," I say before clicking off and going to deal with more talk of flow meters and fill gauges. I sigh and put the phone on the counter. I would rather pick bubble gum out of Dom's hair than talk about copper piping anymore. *Just keep thinking about the nice running water.* I put on my nicest smile and head around the corner.

The plumber finally leaves just as Beau's truck pulls up in front. Mom isn't home yet. She'll be sorry she missed him, I know, but seeing him isn't helping her actually get over him. I know they say it takes half as long as you were in a relationship to get over the relationship, but I'm not sure I can take any more of this. When I open the door, Beau is standing there with Batman and Cinderella. Sort of. Dominic looks normal from the waist down—cargo pants and sneakers—but from the waist up, he's Batman. Lucy, on the other hand, looks like she went through a war where they used lipstick instead of bullets for ammunition.

"Don't I look pretty?" she asks, sliding past me.

"Very," I say. Beau looks like he's also been through a war, but one I'm not sure he's going to survive. "Long weekend?" I ask. There, a tiny piece of me that's glad he's gotten this glimpse of what it means to be a single parent, but most of me wants their visits to go well. Because whether I like him right now or not, he is Dom and Lucy's father. And whether I'm mad at him or not, he is officially my father too, since he adopted me when I was seven.

"They are very high-energy," Beau says. I look up at the ceiling above our heads, which is actually the floor of their bedroom and where they must currently be training elephants to jump through hoops. "So," Beau says, leaning against the doorjamb. "How are you?" I'm surprised at his question. It isn't like him to actually attempt a conversation. Usually he's all about the drop-and-bolt.

I shrug. "Okay, I guess. Busy." He nods and keeps standing there, so I try again. "You know, school, candy making—"

Something in his pocket beeps loudly. He pulls out his phone and looks at it. "I have to go," he says. His voice sounds sad, but maybe he's just tired. I nod. He stands there for a moment, like he's unsure whether he should hug me or shake my hand or something. I just lift my hand as if to wave. He gives me a tired smile and turns to walk down the sidewalk toward his truck. I take a deep breath. My mother isn't the only one who has a hard time seeing Beau. I close the door just in time to hear something very large and very heavy hit the floor above me.

"Dom! Lucy!" I yell in the direction of the stairs. I hear

two sets of feet running toward the hallway, so I reason they are both still alive and at least still have the use of their legs. I decide that I need some food in me before I tackle whatever mess there is upstairs.

I quickly fix a few grilled cheese sandwiches and pour three glasses of milk. I add some apple chunks, knowing that they probably lived on takeout and sugary cereal all weekend. I call for them as I slide the sandwiches out of the frying pan. Lucy comes careening into the room first. She slides into one of the chairs at the kitchen table. The hem of her princess dress catches on the edge of the chair, and I hear a ripping sound as the tulle gives way. Dominic, close on her heels, jostles her briefly. Even though there are three other chairs pushed up to the table, they always want the same one. I plunk a plate of food in front of Lucy and another in front of an empty chair on the other side of the table.

Dominic takes the other chair and immediately starts tearing the crusts off his sandwich. He sneers at the apples, or at least I think he does. The Batman mask makes it hard to tell. "Why can't we have Lucky Charms?" he asks. I resist the urge to pour the glass of milk over his head and instead set it on the table beside his plate.

"Where's Mommy?" Lucy asks, dribbling milk down the front of her princess dress.

"She's at the shop," I say. Dominic tries to push scraps of sandwich through the mouth slit in his mask. I slide the mask up onto the top of his head. He frowns at me, but starts eating his sandwich with his own mouth.

"When's she coming home?" Dominic asks.

"Soon," I say.

"That's what you always say," Dom says. I can't argue with that. He takes one last bite of sandwich before pushing away from the table. His movement upends his glass, sending a river of milk flowing toward Lucy. She screams and tries to get away from the table, tilting her chair so far back that she ends up on the ground and her dinner ends up on top of her.

I decide to move bedtime up about an hour. It only takes me ten minutes, four washcloths, and a round of toothbrush wrestling to get them in bed. They are nearly asleep before I've even gotten them all tucked in. I pull their door closed and head back downstairs, checking the clock on the way. Nearly seven.

I'm about halfway through the dishes when Jillian calls to tell me about the *kickin'* earrings she and Claire found at Jump! I bite the inside of my cheek as she talks. I feel a funny twinge of jealousy at all the time Claire and Jillian have been spending together, but I tell it to be quiet. I've just been busy and Claire needs the company. Jillian starts in on The Plan again, talking about something called a mani-pedi, which I figure out has to do with having our nails done. I just listen and um-hum. At one point I even put the phone on the counter so I can dry the dishes with both hands. When I pick it up again, she's moved on to talking about the truffles. She doesn't even seem to have noticed that I was gone.

Jillian and I agree that we shouldn't force the truffles on the guys. Instead we'll position ourselves with the chocolates and rely on guys' general state of always being hungry to do the rest.

"Piper, you just have to be casual about it," Jillian says. I roll my eyes.

"I got it," I say. Then slowly, as if I'm writing it down, I add, "be casual."

"I'll leave your chocolates in your locker before zero period." Most of us only take six classes, but Jillian goes to school an hour early to take Latin. She might act like a ditz sometimes, but she's anything but stupid. "What are you wearing tomorrow?" she asks finally.

"I don't know. My uniform?"

I can almost hear Jillian's eyes rolling through the phone. "Wear your gray hoodie with the embroidered flowers all over it and your sandals with the vegetables on them. You know, casual chic."

I squint at my reflection in the microwave door. I have never in my life uttered the word *chic* in a non-ironic way. "Listen, Jillian. I've got to go. I still have to finish my lab write-up for biology." I start to say good-bye, but Jillian cuts me off with more beauty advice.

"Make sure you do something with your hair after practice. Don't just let it air dry." I make a note to put my hair dryer in my gym bag.

"Gotcha," I say.

"As for makeup—" I pull the phone away from my mouth.

"Jillian—I'm going to lose you. I'm about to enter a tunnel."

"Tunnel? What tun—" I click the end button on my phone and place it on the counter. I close my eyes for a second. Talking to Jillian makes me tired. The home phone rings and I shake my head. I pick it up and start talking fast.

"Jillian, listen. I really have work to do." There's silence and then the sound of someone clearing his throat. "Hello?"

"Hey there, princess." I suddenly feel cold all over, like someone just dropped me into a pool of ice water. It's weird how just three words can unglue you. Seemingly harmless words that, when delivered by the right person, can cut your heart in two. "You there?" I close my eyes and concentrate. *Just focus on the words,* I tell myself.

"Yes," I say. I say it so softly that I have to repeat it. "Yes, I'm here." I take a deep breath, willing my heart to slow down. Why after all this time is my father calling? "What do you want?" There's more silence. My words came out harsher than I intended, but what does he expect after nearly two whole years?

"I just called to see how you are." My heart starts thumping even harder. I hate my heart for that, like it's betraying me. *Stop it,* I tell it, but it won't listen. "Got a birthday coming up."

"Yeah," I say softly. "I do." I remember my birthday two years ago, sitting alone in front of The Paper Lantern, waiting for him to show up.

"Seems like just yesterday you were blowing out the candles on your Cinderella cake." I close my eyes. Cinderella was when I was six. The silence stretches between us again. Part of me longs for him to fill it, but the rest of me is glad he doesn't even try. "Listen," he says finally. "Is your mom around?" And there it is. I glance at the clock over the kitchen table. We couldn't even make it three minutes.

"She's at the shop," I say. He's quiet again.

"Maybe I'll call her there," he says. "It was good to talk to you, princess." There's more silence. "Listen," he begins. And I do. "We'll talk soon, okay?"

"Okay," I say, hating that little spark of hope that flares up inside of me. There's a click and the line goes dead. I stand there with the phone in my hand until it starts beeping at me to hang it up. I place it on the counter and walk upstairs. I lie on my bed and stare at the ceiling over me. It's the same ceiling I've stared at for eleven years. It's the ceiling I stared at when my parents used to fight—when Jack left, then came back, then left again. It's the same one I stared at when Beau and my mom started dating and then got married and then had Dom and Lucy one right after the other. Like they needed to hurry because the clock was ticking. Which I guess it was. He left when Lucy was only two. That's two dads that walked out on us, walked out on *me*, in less than ten years. *Yeah Charlie,* I whisper to the ceiling. *Maybe I am cynical, but for a good reason.* Maybe instead of trying to find a potion that helps you fall in love, someone should come up with one that makes you *stay* in love. Then you'd really have something.

I feel a blanket being pulled over me. I open my eyes and see my mother standing beside my bed. I squint at the clock. Almost nine. I must have fallen asleep. My mom pushes my hip and I slide over, giving her room to sit beside me on the bed.

"You okay?" she asks. I can feel the heat behind my eyes. Tears that I refuse to let fall. Not over him. Not again. "Jack called the shop. Said he talked to you." I nod.

"What did he want?" I ask.

"I don't really know." She sighs and looks away from me. "He asked me a lot of questions about you." She looks back at me. I raise my eyebrow. "He wanted to know if you're happy."

"What did you tell him?" I ask, not sure what I would have answered if he'd asked me the same thing.

"I told him I thought you were." She looks at me for a long moment. "Was I right?" I poke around inside of myself for a minute before deciding.

"I'm pretty happy," I admit.

She gives me a small smile, then takes a breath. "He also

wants to see you." I close my eyes. She finds my hand under the blanket and squeezes it. Her fingers are cold against mine. "You don't have to," she says. "After all this time, he can't really enforce visitation."

"I'll think about it," I say. My head says no way; it's my heart that needs to think about it.

"He gave me his new number," she says. "I put it on your desk." I look over at the piece of paper sitting there, tucked under my crystal heart paperweight. It's small, just part of a piece of paper, but it seems to push some of the air out of the room. "I was worried," Mom says. "I tried to call the house, but the line was busy." I think of the phone I dropped on the counter without hanging it up. "You didn't answer your cell."

"It's downstairs," I say.

"I was worried," she says again.

"I'm okay," I say. I look at her. She's staring at my face. "Really."

"Pinkie-swear?" she asks. I find her pinkie with mine and squeeze it. "Don't forget to set your alarm. Charlie came over to tell you he'd be out front at ten after and not to be late."

"Charlie came over?" I ask, reaching for my clock. I set it for five A.M. Yuck.

"Apparently he couldn't get through on the phone either." She smiles at me. "He also said good job on the new truffles." She pulls my door shut as she leaves. I put my clock back on the bedside table and pull my biology lab book from my backpack. Just then, what my mother said hits me. I leap out of bed and run out into the hall.

"Which truffles?" I ask.

"The new ones. He said he stopped by Jan's today to see you and he loaded up on free candy." She shakes her head. "It's a wonder that man is able to stay in business with everything he's always giving away."

I smirk. If there is such a thing as a love potion, Jillian will be pretty excited to know that Charlie ate some of our truffles. "Better get to sleep. Big day tomorrow," I say, kissing her fast on the cheek. She smiles and shakes her head at me. I trudge into my room and climb into bed. This is exactly why I wouldn't use magic even if it did exist. There's too much randomness in the world. I'd probably a) cast the wrong spell on b) the wrong person. Ugh. I completely refuse to get caught up in the insanity of Jillian's plan. But, I am in this for as long as Claire is. Like Jillian said, she needs it.

chapter nine

I lean over and tilt my head, trying to get the water out of my ear. I can feel it sloshing around in there. The good news is that our coach still has the same rule from last season. If someone throws up during practice, we get out fifteen minutes early, and if two people lose it, we end practice immediately. The bad news is that this morning, I was the second puker. I let Charlie talk me into drinking some new protein shake his coach recommended. It's horrible, full of spirulina and kelp. It tasted bad enough going down. It was worse coming back up.

"Nice work, Paisley!" I look over and see Peter (Mr. Row Butt) giving me the thumbs-up. I wave at him weakly. I can still taste the seaweed in my mouth. He walks over to where a girl with long blond hair is leaning down from the bleachers, waiting to talk to him. She giggles at something he says.

"Didn't take him long," I mutter, picking up the stack of kickboards. Another of coach's rules. The pukers get to do cleanup.

"Didn't take who long to do what?" I look over to where someone is kicking half a dozen pull buoys toward the storage bin.

I feel a flutter in my stomach that isn't the seaweed. It's Ben Donovan. "Umm . . ." I can be so witty under pressure.

Ben looks over to where Peter is still flirting with the blonde. "He's really broken up about you guys," he says. I shake my head and hide a smile, both because he's being so nice to me and because Ben Donovan actually noticed I was going out with Peter.

"He's brave to hide it so well," I say.

"Crying on the inside." Ben Donovan leans over and picks up one of the pull buoys and chucks it at the back of Peter's head. "Hey, Pete. You owe me breakfast." Peter smiles over at him and shakes his head. "It's your fault I urped," Ben Donovan says.

"Dude, it's not my fault you didn't train over break," Peter says.

Ben Donovan looks over at me. "Does he owe you breakfast, too?" I shrug. "Hey, Pete, you owe Piper here breakfast, too."

Peter acts like he's about to make a smart remark at my expense, but he looks over at the blonde who's still admiring him like he's Adonis in a Speedo. "You hungry?" he asks her.

She nods, but she seems uncertain. I can't help rolling my eyes. Another girl who can't eat in front of guys. I dump the last pile of kickboards in the bin and heft my bag from where I put it against the wall.

Ben Donovan walks toward the locker room and I wonder if any of that was real or just guy talk. He catches the door and turns to look at me. "Meet us in the caff in ten," he says.

"I have to drop by my locker," I say, then realize with a smirk that this might be the perfect time to *casually* give him the chocolates.

"Okay, then in twelve." He winks at me, which makes my heart thud a little harder. "I'll save you a seat."

I hurry through my shower and pull on my uniform. I say a silent thanks to Jillian that she had her little fashion meeting with me. It takes me three minutes to blow-dry my hair. I start to put on some of the lipstick I dropped in my bag at the last minute, but decide against it. I don't want to look like I'm trying too hard. I grab my bag and start toward my locker. The halls are still mostly empty, just a few students here and there putting up flyers and wandering around. I twist my combination and pull my locker open, expecting to see my usual messy jumble of books and a couple of boxes of chocolates, but there's also something else. Hanging from one of the hooks meant to hold jackets is a small brown bag. I pull it down and peer inside.

"A banana," I say out loud. I pull it out and look at it. It's perfect. Just this side of green and no spots. Maybe Jillian thought I'd need something to eat after practice. I unload my backpack and lay the banana carefully on the stack of books inside. Smiling, I grab one of the boxes of chocolates and snap my locker shut. I might as well give them to Ben Donovan now since I know Jillian will ask. But when I start heading toward the caff, I'm suddenly nervous. This morning was the longest conversation I've ever had with Ben Donovan. What if I don't have anything more to say? What if I just sit there like a lump while he mentally kicks himself for inviting such a hopeless girl to have breakfast with him? By the time I round the corner, I feel more like I'm walking to the gallows than to breakfast.

Sitting on the far side of the caff in one of the booths are Peter and Ben Donovan. The blonde girl Peter was talking to is walking toward them, balancing two trays. One has four cups of coffee on it; the other is heaped with plates. I watch her wobble a little, then I hurry to her rescue. She hands me one of the trays with a grateful smile and I walk with her over to where the guys are sitting.

"Hey there," Ben Donovan says, sliding over to make room for me. The smart remark I had about treating women like servants dies when he smiles at me. I put my tray on the table along with the box of chocolates. Peter introduces the blonde as Susan, who quickly corrects him.

"It's Sarah," she says, putting her tray on the table and sitting down.

"Right. Sarah, I meant Sarah." But Peter is only half

paying attention because he's already pulling open the box of chocolates.

"Is this what I think it is?" He pulls back the tissue paper and peers inside. "Awesome," he says. "Can I have one?" he asks, looking up at me. I'm stuck. It's not like I can say *Um, no actually they are for Ben Donovan and not someone who can't even pronounce robot.*

"Sure," I say. He grabs two and drops them into his mouth one after the other.

"Dude," he says, closing his eyes. "You have got to try these." Ben Donovan takes one. I hold my breath, watching, thinking what if the love potion does work? Then I check myself. This is reality. In reality as I know it, there's no such thing as magic. I look over at Peter as he starts shoveling forkfuls of pancakes into his mouth. Okay, so in addition to being sort of moronic, he also has terrible manners.

"Piper, these are awesome," Ben Donovan says, reaching for another truffle. I take a sip of my coffee and smile at him. I needn't have worried about what to talk about. The next several minutes are devoted to the guys shoving as much food into their mouths as they can in the shortest amount of time possible. I look over at Sarah, who seems too taken with Peter to be bothered by his gluttony. In addition to eating their own breakfasts, they inhale most of mine and Sarah's. The guys finish off their feast with the rest of my box of chocolates. They offer one to Sarah, who shakes her head primly, as if *she couldn't possibly.*

"So, Piper," Peter says, leaning back and looking at me. "Whose heart are you breaking now?"

I roll my eyes at him, but I'm aware that Ben Donovan is looking at me too. "I am currently unattached," I say, pretending to be much cooler than I feel.

Peter smirks at me, then looks over at Ben Donovan. "Dude, watch out. She's ruthless." I feel my cheeks heating up. It's all I can do to avoid looking over to see his reaction.

"I'll take that under advisement," he says. I peek at him out of the corner of my eye and see him smiling at me. Peter just laughs and puts his arm around Sarah, who looks like she's about to dissolve into a puddle of happiness. Luckily the bell signaling the end of zero period sounds, saving me from having to actually say anything. Sarah stacks the trays and gets up to return them. And of course the guys let her. Someone needs to tell her to stop being so servile.

"Thanks for breakfast, Peter," I say. He just shrugs. I know money is nothing to him. His family is loaded.

The four of us head out to the hall, where we split off toward our various homerooms. I only make it about a dozen steps away before I hear my name behind me. I turn and look at Ben Donovan, standing there with a grin on his face. I notice that everyone else within earshot has turned and is looking at him too.

"See you around." He smiles at me then walks away down the hall, parting the crowds in front of him. All eyes are on me. Everyone wants to know who Ben Donovan is going to "see around." I feel myself blushing all the way down into my veggie sandals. I walk to my locker, hyperaware that people are still gawking at me. I open my locker, grab my perfect banana and pull out my books. It isn't until I spot the other box of chocolates that I pause. What if—but I snap my locker shut before I can even finish the thought. If there were magic in the world, I'm pretty sure it wouldn't exist in Atlanta. Seriously.

"And then what did he say?" Jillian asks. General school craziness kept me from talking to Jillian and Claire all day long. I even spent lunchtime in the library getting a head start on my Brit lit midterm paper. I called them to tell them the details as soon as I got home, but Jillian told me to wait—they'd be right over. Luckily Mrs. Bateman is over her cold, so she can watch Dom and Lucy, giving me more time (and some peace and quiet) to actually get my schoolwork done.

I'm nearly through my lab report for biology when they arrive. We grab juice from the fridge (orange, not acai) and head up to my room. We're barely through the door before Jillian starts firing questions at me. I try to answer, but she's asking them so fast, I can't get a word in.

Claire holds up her hand, silencing Jillian. "Tell us everything," she says.

I start with explaining our coach's rule about throwing up during practice and end where Ben Donovan told me he'd see me around. It takes forever to tell them the whole thing because Jillian keeps interrupting to ask random questions, like "What was Ben Donovan wearing?" and "Did he smile when he ate the truffle?" They both seem most interested in whether I think the spell worked or not.

"No," I say. Then I see the look on Claire's face and I amend my answer. "I don't know. Maybe." The light goes back on in Claire's eyes. Maybe I'm just being grouchy. Even I have to admit that there's something going on. I mean, why after nearly two and a half years of high school does Ben Donovan suddenly pick today of all days to notice me? And yet, he noticed me *before* he ate the chocolates. I don't draw attention to that part, reminding myself that Claire needs this.

"So what about you guys?" I ask. "How did it go with you?" Claire starts laughing immediately and I'm surprised to see Jillian blush a little. "What?" I ask, feeling left out. It takes a minute before Claire can compose herself enough to actually speak.

"So during lunch, we're sitting in our normal spot near the windows." I nod. "And suddenly Jillian gets up." Claire starts laughing again. "Brett and Sam were sitting by themselves over near the coffee bar." I nod again. "So she just walks right over to them sits down at their table." I look over at Jillian, who shrugs.

"What did they do?" I ask.

"At first they seemed surprised," Jillian says. *I'll bet,* I'm thinking. "But then I put the box of chocolates on the table. That got their attention."

"So that wasn't weird? Just walking up and giving them candy?" I ask.

"To a girl, yes. But guys are all about their stomachs." Remembering the scene at breakfast, I nod.

"Then what happened?" I ask.

Jillian frowns. "That's when their girlfriends showed up."

"Ouch," I say. "What did they say?"

Jillian shrugs. "I got out of there. I didn't want some big drama."

"Tell her the rest," Claire says, still smiling. I look over at Jillian, but she doesn't say anything. "So then we spent the rest of lunch watching *the girlfriends* feed Brett and Sam Jillian's chocolates," Claire says. I look back at Jillian, a little worried that she might be upset about it. The Plan was her idea after all, but she just waves her hand.

"It was a long shot," she says. I wait for more explanation, but she just looks away. There is definitely something fishy about how Jillian is acting.

"Claire, tell Piper about you," Jillian says, obviously trying to change my focus. It works. I look over at Claire. I know she was worried about giving the candy to Stuart. If I were Stuart I'd worry. Worry that they were poisoned. But Claire's not that girl. She's too nice.

"I dropped them off before rugby practice," she says. "At first I was just going to give Alex his, but Stuart was right

there and I pretended like it was no big deal, like I had ex-
tras so he might as well have them." She looks down at her
hands.

"Was it hard to see him?" I ask softly. She nods, but won't
look up at me. Tears fall onto the pillow she has cradled in
her lap.

"I'm sorry," she says. She pushes the pillow to the floor
and hurries out of the room. I hear the bathroom door
shut behind her. Jillian and I don't say anything for a few
moments.

"Maybe this isn't such a good idea," I say quietly so Claire
won't overhear.

Jillian looks over at me and for the first time I see doubt in
her eyes. "What else can we do?" she asks.

"Wait it out," I say, but I think of my mother and how long
it's taking her to finally let go of Beau. I sigh. "She needs a
distraction."

"Like what?" Jillian asks.

There I'm at a loss. My phone barks. My mother. I pick it
up. "Hello?" I say. It's loud on her end. Voices and the whir
of fans.

"Piper, I'm going to be late again," she says. "I've already
talked to Mrs. Bateman. She's going to get Dom and Lucy
ready for bed over there."

"It's okay, Mom. You don't have to pay her for that. I'll
watch them." My mother sighs and I can see her, fighting
with herself, biting her lip.

"You sure?" she asks finally.

"I'm sure. I'll just keep adding to that *You Owe Me* list I have going."

She laughs. "It might be a long list before this season is out."

Suddenly inspiration strikes. "Mom, why don't you get some help?"

"I don't have the time to find someone and then train them. And I can't trust just *anyone* to take on some of this stuff." The voices get louder and I hear my mother say something to someone there in the shop. "I have to go, Piper. I'll call Mrs. Bateman back. Thank you again."

"No problem," I say, but the line is already dead. I toss the phone on the bed and look over at Jillian. "I am about to solve two problems with one stone."

"Don't you mean kill two birds with one stone?" Jillian asks.

"Yes, but that's cruel." She laughs and tosses a pillow at me. We hear the door to the bathroom open and Claire comes around the corner. She's stopped crying, but her eyes are red and she's sniffling into a tissue.

"I have the best idea in the whole world," I say. Claire raises her eyebrows at me. I quickly explain that my mother needs help at the shop and I think it would really be good if she had something to do other than miss Stuart.

"I think it's an excellent idea," Jillian says. It sort of makes me mad that Claire seems unsure until Jillian says that.

Like my opinion isn't quite enough to make her consider it. "And," Jillian says, drawing out the word, "being around all those flowers and all that romance is definitely going to get you in the Valentine's Day spirit." Why do I have the feeling that a new phase of The Plan is in the works?

"Did your mom okay this?" Claire asks.

"Oh, she will. My mother loves you," I say. What I don't say is that love her or not, my mother is desperate. Claire nods and gives one more sniff before reaching to throw her tissue in the trash. In the process, she accidentally knocks my heart paperweight off the desk. Papers go everywhere, and even though I tell her not to worry about it, she scrambles to pick them up. She picks up the last paper and looks at it.

"Jack?" she asks. It's the slip of paper with my father's phone number on it. I just nod. "Are you going to call him?" she asks.

"I'm thinking about it." What I mean is that I'm trying not to think about it, but not succeeding very well.

"Who's Jack?" Jillian asks. Before I can answer, she continues. "Is he cute?" I sigh, but then there's a loud thump on the roof, saving me from answering.

Jillian doesn't scream this time. She just jumps up, runs to my window and sticks her head out. "Hi, Charlie," she says. I can't hear exactly what he says, but I can hear his tone of voice and he sounds more than a little nervous. Jillian's intensity can make anyone a little nervous.

"Tell him to come over," I say, taking some pity on him. She tells him and pulls her head back in. Her eyes are shiny and her cheeks are flushed.

She sighs and pretends to fan herself like she's Scarlett in *Gone with the Wind* or something. "He sure is yummy." She is halfway out the door when she turns and looks at us. "Too bad we don't have any more candy," she says.

"Yes," I say, remembering that Charlie already had some of it last night. "It is too bad." Jillian starts down the stairs. I wait for Claire. I don't know what else to say, so I just take her arm and give it a squeeze. We walk downstairs like that, arm in arm, and I feel a little like Scarlett myself, although our staircase is carpeted and narrow and I'm wearing jeans and a Jan the Candy Man shirt. And Claire is no Rhett Butler. I shake my head, wondering if all the romance in the air is making my brain mushy.

chapter ten

I watch Jillian and Charlie the whole time they're together, trying to see Charlie the way she sees him. Jillian's pretty much the same, only intensified. She tosses her hair around so much, I'm afraid she's going to get whiplash. Charlie is like he always is too: nice and vaguely oblivious.

Jillian and Claire leave pretty much as soon as Lucy and Dom arrive. Not that I blame them. Those two know how to clear a room. Charlie asks if he can stay.

"Of course you can. I figured your dad was in the middle of something big," I say

"Sort of," Charlie says, not looking at me.

I start to ask what "sort of" means, but Dom starts yelling from the other room that he's *starving*. I take a package of spaghetti from the pantry. Thinking about how much Charlie usually eats, I grab two.

Charlie sneaks a handful of baby carrots from the bag on the counter and starts munching on them. While I put a pot of water on to boil, I tell him about barfing in the pool and about how Peter had to buy me breakfast.

"You break up with him and then you make him buy you breakfast?" Charlie laughs. "Classic. I would have given a lot to have seen that." Charlie doesn't hide the fact that he's not a big fan of the guys on the swim team at my school. I always tell him that he'd probably like them if he got to know them individually, but all he knows of them is when they are all together. It's like one big testosterone fest. It's not pretty. I start to tell him about Ben Donovan, but he's not listening anymore. He's staring out the window toward his house. "Charlie?"

"What?"

I tilt my head at him, but he just looks away. There is a big crash upstairs, then Miss Kitty shoots through the room like she has a string of firecrackers tied to her tail, which thankfully she does not. "Would you mind?" I ask, pointing at the ceiling where I can hear Dom and Lucy stomping around.

"No problem," Charlie says. He grabs another handful of carrots and heads upstairs.

I smirk. "So he says."

About halfway through boiling the pasta, I hear loud music start upstairs. I shake my head and finish setting the table. I call my mother at the shop, but it clicks over to voice mail. Either she's too busy to pick up the phone or she's on her way home. I set a fifth place for her, hoping for the latter. After draining the pasta, I go to the bottom of the stairs and yell that dinner is ready, but the music is too loud for me to be heard. I climb the stairs, unsure of what I'm going to find. I round the corner toward Dom and Lucy's bedroom and stop, just watching. I smile, but it quickly becomes laughter. And it's not Dominic's wild jumping or Lucy's imitation of a whirling dervish that makes me laugh, but Charlie's strange gyrations that make him look like a cross between a salmon swimming upstream and a scarecrow with its head on fire.

Dom sees me first and waves. Lucy collapses on the floor and starts giggling, leaving Charlie to dance alone. I can't stop laughing and it's not just Charlie's weird dancing, it's him, how he always is with my little brother and sister. Charlie never bolts when they're around. In fact, it's the opposite. He actually seems genuinely bummed when they're gone. I watch him for several more moments before taking pity on him.

"Hey!" I yell. He stops mid-twirl and looks over to where I'm standing. His face turns as red as the tomato sauce I was heating up.

"Not a word," he says, pointing toward me. I start laughing again, so hard this time that tears spring to my eyes. He walks over to the stereo and turns the music way down.

"Isn't Charlie a great dancer?" Lucy asks.

I nod, trying to catch my breath. Charlie shakes his head

and smiles at me, pushing his hair out of his eyes. "He is a very interesting dancer," I say. Lucy nods, smiling. Lucy has a crush on Charlie. She frequently tells me that she is going to marry him. When she gets old, *like eighteen*. I don't have the heart to remind her that when she's eighteen, Charlie will be *really old*. Over thirty.

"Dinner is ready," I say. "Unless you guys want to keep dancing."

"Charlie loves to dance," Lucy says, walking over to take his hand. She looks up at him expectantly.

"I love to dance with you, Lucy-lu," he says. He throws her over his shoulder, making her squeal. Then he goes for Dom, who bolts out from under his grasp and heads for the stairs and freedom. Charlie walks downstairs carrying Lucy over his shoulder like a sack of potatoes.

"Thanks," I say, and I don't mean just for the dancing. It's bigger than that. Charlie's had dozens of tea parties with Lucy and played hours of LEGOs with Dom. He has no idea what that means to them. To Mom. To me.

"They're fun," Charlie says. "Course now I think I need to take a nap."

I smirk. "He can bust out a three-hour workout in the pool, but fifteen minutes with these two and he's down for the count."

"They have a lot of energy."

I laugh. "If that's code for they are the spawn of the devil, then yes, they have a lot of energy."

"I'm not the debil," Lucy says, her voice nasally from hanging upside down.

I ruffle her hair. "No," I say. "You're not the debil."

Mom arrives just as I'm dishing up the plates. She sinks into one of the chairs and sighs. "Long day?" I ask. She nods and accepts a plate of pasta with a smile. We eat as she tells us about this woman who came into the shop demanding blue roses.

"I just kept telling her there's no such thing, but she refused to believe me. She said she saw a painting of one." Mom shakes her head. Lucy tells us she's going to grow blue roses. "Do you think you can do that before Valentine's Day?" my mother asks, smiling.

Lucy looks serious for a moment. "If I do, will you be home more?" she asks. Mom smiles at her, but her eyes are sad. She opens her arms toward Lucy, who climbs into her lap. I can tell Mom doesn't know what to say. I mean, I hate it that she's gone all the time too, but I can understand why. Supporting three kids on your own is hard, especially when all your money comes from flowers. I start clearing the table. Charlie helps by finishing up the rest of the pasta, eating it straight out of the strainer in the sink.

"So how's the training going?" Mom asks Charlie.

He shrugs. "Good." I shake my head as I rinse off the dishes. Even when Charlie broke three state records his sophomore year, he still said "good." I'll bet he could make the Olympic team and still he'd keep it to himself. Mom smiles too but doesn't press him. Charlie always seems so embarrassed when he has to talk about himself.

"Are you still seeing Julie?" Mom asks. I look over at Charlie.

"We decided that we make better friends," he says.

"So she dumped you?" I ask.

"No, Pipe. Unlike when you say it, sometimes people actually mean it." I flick some bubbles at him. "Is it okay if I just hang here for a while?" he asks my mom.

"Of course, Charlie. You are always welcome here," she says. "Sure your dad won't want you home?" Charlie looks over in the direction of his house for a long moment, then shakes his head.

"He's busy," he says. He slides a box of chocolates out of the cabinet over the fridge and sits at the table. He rummages in his backpack and pulls out his notebook and a textbook that has ORGANIC CHEMISTRY printed on the spine.

I resolve to ask him why he's acting so weird about his father next time we're alone. I'm scrubbing the pot I heated the sauce in when I start hearing seagulls and the crashing of ocean waves. I look up, trying to figure out where the noise is coming from, but then I see Charlie grinning. I look at my cell, which is peeking out of the front pocket of my backpack.

"I'll get it," says Dom, sliding down from the table.

"No, just—" I begin, but it's too late. Dom already has my phone to his ear.

"What do you want?" he asks. Someone needs to work on

his phone manners. My mother tries to take the phone from him, but he scoots out of her reach. Finally Dom extends the phone toward me. "It's for you." I smirk and resist the urge to say *duh*. "It's a boy."

"Ooooo," Lucy says from my mother's lap loud enough for the person on the phone to hear. I quickly dry my hands and reach for the phone, looking at the screen. I don't recognize the number. Instantly I feel sort of wobbly. I try to remember the number printed on the slip of paper still sitting on my desk upstairs, but I can't.

"Hello?" I say, hesitantly. I avoid looking at anyone else in the room, especially my mother.

"Hello?" the voice on the other end says. "Piper?" It's not my father, which makes my heart start thudding a little less.

"Yes," I say. "Who's this?"

"It's Ben," the voice says, which of course makes my heart start up again. "Is this a bad time? I mean I can—"

"No," I say, turning to walk into the living room where I can maybe have a tiny bit of privacy. "It's fine."

"Peter gave me your number," Ben Donovan says. "I hope you don't mind."

Don't mind? I think. I can't imagine anyone minding if Ben Donovan called. "No," I say. "I don't mind."

"I just wanted to call and see if you wanted to hang out this weekend."

I start to say no, because even if Ben Donovan is my ideal, I just don't date. But then I remember Charlie calling me cynical and Claire begging me to go along with The Plan. I take a breath. "Sure," I say all casual, like getting asked out by someone like Ben Donovan happens all the time to someone like me.

"Cool," Ben Donovan says. "After the meet then," he says.

I nod, but then remember that this is a phone and he can't see my head move. "Yeah," I say.

"Cool," Ben Donovan says again. "See you tomorrow then," he says. All I can do is keep nodding, but it's okay this time because he's already hung up. I stare at the phone in my hand and then tap "Save number" and type in B-e-n-D-o-n-o-v-a-n. I look at my phone until the screen goes dark. *I am now a girl with Ben Donovan's number in my phone. No wait,* I think. *I am now a girl who is going on a date with Ben Donovan.* I feel disconnected from myself. It's like I'm watching myself to see what I'll do next.

"Piper?" my mother says. I look up and see her looking at me from the doorway. "Is everything okay?"

"Yes," I say. "Everything is okay."

"I'm going to get the kids to bed," she says. I hear her shepherding Dom and Lucy up the stairs.

I walk out to the kitchen and slide my books from my backpack. I sit across the table from Charlie and open my notebook. Charlie looks at me, his eyebrows raised, but I just give him a big smile. I try to make it through the reading for Brit lit, but I'm so distracted that I give up and slide out my biology book and a box of colored pencils. We have to color in the digestive system. Coloring I can do. I'm trying to figure out how I feel about agreeing to go out with Ben Donovan. Any other girl at Montrose would be dancing through her house, having already called her friends and told them. Me? I'm doing homework.

"So, who's the new guy?" Charlie asks, without looking up from his homework.

"No one you know," I say. It's a tiny lie. Charlie knows who Ben Donovan *is*.

Charlie looks up at me. "Just be careful," he says.

"Always," I say, sliding a blue pencil out of the box.

"I mean it," Charlie says.

"You can stop with the big brother stuff," I say. "I'm good."

"I'm not trying to be your big brother, Piper," Charlie says. I look back at him, but he's staring down at his textbook. Even though he's not looking at me, I can tell he's blushing. I shake my head and start outlining the pulmonary veins in blue. Charlie is definitely acting weird. I switch to red to color in the arteries.

"Hush," Charlie says from the other side of the table.

"What?" I ask, looking up.

"You're humming." He shakes his head and looks back at his textbook.

"Sorry," I say. I stop humming aloud, but I can't stop the song from sliding around inside my brain. I don't recognize the tune, but I'm sure Jan would. I'm pretty sure it's Sinatra.

♡ ♡ ♡

The next few days run one into another. Swim practice, homework, working at Jan's. Mom is home more thanks to Claire's help. And Claire seems way better. I've only seen her tear up once and that was when we saw Stuart holding Christi's hand on the front lawn. Jillian's new idea has been to teach Claire and me how to flirt. She forced me to give my second box of chocolates to Andrew Spence (my plan B) in person. I tried the eye gazing, the giggle, the arm touching. I tried to do the hair toss thing that Jillian taught me, but all I did was whack my head on the edge of his locker door. I got out of there as fast as I could after that. I'm pretty sure the impression I left on Andrew was less cute girl who might make a good Valentine and more irrational mental patient who could possibly be dangerous. I told Jillian that I wasn't going to participate in any more of her flirting seminars.

Jillian has been going into overdrive, leaving little presents in my locker almost every day. I guess the gifts are just Jillian's way of trying to get me into the spirit. Tuesday's bag contained a jar of peanut butter and a plastic spoon. Then there was a pin that read BE QUIET. I CAN'T HEAR THE VOICES IN MY HEAD. I actually laughed out loud when I read it, making people in the hall look at me funny. Then there's a windup toy cockroach that I can't wait to show Dom.

The closer we get to the weekend, the more Claire and Jillian want to talk about my date with Ben Donovan. I'm trying to match their enthusiasm by imagining how other girls would be acting if they were going out with him. Jillian tells me I'm *the ultimate average-girl hero*. I'm not sure I like being called a hero and even less an average girl.

Jan texts me to say that my Consternation Hearts are selling so well he decided we need to order more. I drop by the shop after school to help box up all the stock we have left.

"I'm just not sure how I feel about this," Jan says, after the door closes behind a woman who just bought two dozen boxes of them. I brace myself for another one of Jan's fatherly moments. Sometimes his whole paternal thing makes me crazy, but I know he means well.

"What do you mean?" I ask. "I thought you'd be psyched."

"I don't know," Jan says, straightening the boxes of taffy on top of the glass case. "I mean, I'm really happy that your candy is selling so well, but it just seems sort of—" He leaves off and looks out the window for a moment. "Cynical," he finishes quietly.

"Cynical?" I ask, bristling at the word being tossed in my direction again. "I just thought they were funny."

"Oh, they are," Jan says, smiling at me. "It's just that . . . I don't know . . . Valentine's Day is supposed to be hopeful, you know? Love and romance and all that." He takes off his glasses and polishes them with a handkerchief he takes from his pocket. He puts them back on and looks at me. "I just don't want you to be cynical about love," he says.

"I'm not cynical," I say. "I'm just realistic."

"You want to make sure it's a safe bet before you put your heart on the table."

"Okay, other than that being the world's worst metaphor, yes. Exactly."

"Piper—" Jan begins.

I hold my hand up. "Before you start, you should know that I have a date this weekend."

That makes Jan smile. "Tell me," he says, so I do. In between customers I tell him all about Ben Donovan. "Well, Piper. There might just be hope for you yet."

"Gee thanks," I say, rolling my eyes. "But what about you? You're single. Youngish. And you're not ugly—"

"Nice," Jan says, shaking his head at me.

"Why have I never heard about you going on a date?"

Jan takes a deep breath and looks back out the window. "I guess I'm just not—" He pauses to polish his glasses again. I don't know anything about Jan's past, other than the fact that he used to be married and he has a daughter a little older than me who is in college in California. He looks back at me. "I guess I'm just not quite ready," he says. I wait for him to say more, but he just nods as if that settles it and walks over to the jukebox and selects another song. "Crazy" by Patsy Cline. I smile at him as he waltzes toward the back of the store, pushes through the swinging doors, and disappears.

chapter eleven

I slide three truffles into the box, one each of peppermint, raspberry, and cinnamon. The order just said to box up anything red. I was tempted to add in some of the ancho chili ones until Jeremy tried one. His eyes started watering almost immediately and even after drinking about a gallon of water, he still can't talk above a whisper. "How many is that?" I ask Jillian, who is helping put the little boxes into bigger boxes to be delivered later to a fund-raiser.

"Seventy-eight," Jillian says, tucking in another box.

"And we need how many?" I ask, even though I already know the answer.

"Two hundred and fifty," Jillian says. Jan was happy when Jillian's mom, who is also the president of the Umlaut Foundation, ordered boxes of truffles as favors for their fund-raiser, but Jillian's mom keeps calling every few hours and upping the total as the RSVPs roll in.

I hold up one of the Love Potion No. 9 truffles. "I guess these were a bust."

"Maybe they aren't strong enough," Jillian says. "Or maybe—"

"Maybe there's nothing strong enough to make someone love you," I say. I brace myself for another lecture about my cynicism, but Jillian just shrugs.

"It was worth a shot," she says, smiling at me. I smile back. That is one of the best things about Jillian. Nothing fazes her. She's always positive.

I close one of the boxes and look at it before I hand it off to Jillian. An embossed silver seal with the name of the foundation is on the top. "Who is Umlaut?" I ask. "And why does he or she have a foundation?"

Jillian smirks at me. "An Umlaut is that pair of dots that they put over letters in some German words." I raise my eyebrows at her. "Seriously." She starts on a new box, unfolding it and taping the bottom closed. "It's actually not as lame as it sounds."

"That should be their motto. The Umlaut Foundation. We're not as lame as we sound."

Jillian laughs. "They actually do some cool stuff. Every year the Umlaut Foundation features a *Need to Know* artist from Atlanta at their fund-raiser. Last year it was Kiki Bird."

"She's the one who does the thing with the shoes, isn't she?" I ask.

"See?" Jillian says. "It's a pretty big deal for an artist to be selected."

"Are you going?" I ask.

Jillian rolls her eyes. "I'm trying to get out of it."

"It might be fun," I say.

"Yeah," she says. She purses her lips and gestures toward the wall. "Excellent use of color." She makes her voice lower. "Superb use of negative space." She rolls her eyes at me. "These things are excruciating."

"Maybe the art will be good," I say, trying to salvage something for her. "Who is it this year?" I ask.

Jillian shrugs. "Some painter. He does these huge landscapes with found objects."

I nod then look back over at her. "What's the artist's name?" I ask.

"Frank something. I don't remember."

"Is it Frank Wishman?" I ask.

She nods. "How did you know?"

I smile. I am very familiar with the paintings she's talking about. "Frank Wishman is Charlie's dad," I say.

"Really?" Jillian says, drawing the word out so it sounds like it has eight syllables instead of two. I squint at her. She smiles at me like the Cheshire Cat.

I look around to make sure Jeremy isn't listening. "What about the *hottie* who sits in front of you in chem?"

She just waves her fingers at me. "Piper, do you realize that there are only nine more days until Valentine's Day?"

♥ **love?** maybe.

"Um yeah," I say, thinking of the big sign in Jan's window where he's been counting down to V-Day since the beginning of the month.

"Then you can understand why I'm keeping more than one plate spinning." I nod, but something about her calling Charlie a plate that she's spinning makes me feel slightly protective of him. I start to tell her that Charlie isn't just *some plate*, but she already has her phone to her ear.

"Mom," she says. "I want to go." She pauses, listening. "I just changed my mind. That's all." She looks at me. "How many badges can I have?" She listens again. "I need five, including me." She smiles at me and nods, listening again. "Okay, I'll ask." She pulls the phone away from ear. "Can we do three hundred?" she asks, pointing to the truffles.

"I don't know," I say. "I'll have to ask Jan." I walk to the front of the store where Jeremy is helping Jan refill the bins of hard candy. "She wants three hundred," I tell Jan.

He rolls his eyes then smiles. "Okay, but it's going to clean us out."

"You should start packing up the Love Potion Number Nine truffles," Jeremy says.

Jan smiles at him. "I knew there was a reason I pay you the big bucks."

"You don't pay me," Jeremy says.

"Right," Jan says. "I guess we should fix that." I shake my head and walk back into the kitchen, leaving Jeremy and Jan to negotiate. I nod at Jillian, who relays the information to her mother, then hangs up the phone.

"We're in," she says, smiling at me. "You can bring Ben Donovan, and Claire—well, we'll figure out something for Claire."

"I don't know," I say. "I mean, I'm not sure I—"

"Piper, look. Maybe the irony of all this is lost on you, but I think it's the least you can do for Claire and me."

"The irony?" I ask.

Jillian rolls her eyes at me. "Don't you think it's a *little* ironic that the one person who couldn't care less about romance or anything vaguely love-related is the only one of us that has a solid prospect for Valentine's Day?"

I sigh and start folding another one of the truffle boxes and affixing the silver seal to the top. Why is it that the more I try to duck the whole Valentine's Day thing, the more everyone around me seems to be conspiring against me? "Fine," I say. "I'm in."

Jillian smiles at me. "I'm going to call Claire right now." She pokes at her phone. I decide that I need a little fresh air. I push open the back door and walk out to the alley. I lean against the wall and close my eyes. Jillian's wrong. It isn't that I don't care about love. I do. It's just not for me. I mean, I like the idea of love. I know it makes you feel warm and sort of floaty, but I know what's on the other side of that floaty feeling. I've seen it in my mother's eyes when Jack left and when Beau decided he'd rather have a girlfriend than a wife. I saw it in Claire's eyes when Stuart thought he needed someone new to hold hands with. I saw it in Charlie's dad when Mrs. Wishman decided she needed to have a new life three thousand miles away from her husband and son. And even though I've never had my heart broken by a guy, I've felt enough of that empty, hard feeling you get in your stomach when someone who you believed in and trusted and loved just disappears. So, no thank you. I'll just keep my heart where it is, where it's safe.

I take a deep breath. It's going to be a long night. There are hundreds of truffles to make. There are Consternation Hearts to box up. And apparently there are at least two people counting on me to pull it together enough to keep their Valentine's hopes alive. I push away from the wall, taking one more look out into the quickly darkening sky. It's too bright here under the lights to see the stars, but I say a wish anyway. "I wish . . ." I whisper, but I don't know how to finish.

I walk back into the kitchen, where Jillian is trying not to laugh at Jeremy, who has donned a headband with flashing heart lights sticking up from it. Jan has on an identical headband. Jillian is fiddling with hers. Only one of the hearts will stay lit.

"Hey, Piper," Jan says. "Where's your Valentine's Day spirit?" He hands me a headband and I turn on the lights, watching them blink. I slip my headband on my head, feeling the hearts bouncing on their springs.

"I think my heart's defective," Jillian says. I have to force myself to smile when Jan looks at me. I get the joke, but for some reason it just isn't funny right now.

"I can fix that," Jeremy says, taking Jillian's headband from her. He pulls out the battery and looks at the wires that run from it. He twists one of them a little with his fingers and reinserts the battery.

"You are so nerdy," Jillian says. I look over at her. It's not what she said, but how she said it. It almost sounded like a compliment. "Yay," Jillian says, when he flips the switch and both hearts stay lit. Jillian takes the headband from him and slips it on. She wobbles her head, making them clack together. "Jeremy," she says, grinning at him. "You fixed my broken heart." Both Jan and Jeremy laugh. All I can do is give that same half smile. Jan looks at me for a long moment, but I just shake my head at him. I know I already have a reputation for cynicism in all matters of love. I don't need to state the obvious.

Claire comes by after helping my mom close up the flower shop. She rolls up her sleeves, dons a pair of plastic gloves, and starts helping stuff truffles into boxes. As she does, she tells us about all the weird orders that she's been taking at the shop.

"Some guy ordered twelve dozen roses for his wife. That's one hundred and forty-four roses," she explains, as if we can't do the math.

"Now *that* is romantic," Jillian says.

"Seems desperate to me," I say. Everyone looks at me. "Oh, come on. Twelve dozen? That's a little over the top."

"I once bought six dozen roses for my wife," Jan says.

"Why only six?" I ask. "Why not twelve?" I smirk at him, but he just looks at me for a moment before going back to stirring the bowl of chocolate he has melting on the stove. Suddenly the kitchen feels really small.

Jeremy looks from me to Jan then back at the truffles he's packaging. "I think sending some chick one hundred and forty-four roses is a bold move. As I always say: Go big or go home."

Jillian snorts. "Exactly when do you say that?"

"Well, now for one," Jeremy says. Jillian shakes her head, but she can't help smiling. "Oh," Jeremy explains, making us all look at him. "Jan, I have the best idea for next month." Jan looks over at Jeremy, but not before catching my eye and smiling a little. I let out the breath I was holding and resolve to keep my negativity to myself.

"Tell me," Jan says.

"Bacon."

"Bacon?" Jan tilts his head to one side.

"Everyone likes bacon," Jeremy says. He looks at all of us. Jillian and Claire nod and I cast my vote too, nodding along with them. "And everyone likes chocolate."

"Hmm," Jan says. He keeps stirring the bowl of choco-late. "Bacon truffles." Jan smiles over at us. "You guys are

really earning your pay today." Jillian and Claire both protest that he doesn't actually pay them anything, making Jan
laugh. He stops stirring and lifts the bowl from the stove.
He pours the chocolate onto the marble slab set into the
counter and begins folding it in on itself over and over with
a long spatula.

Jan instructs Jeremy to order sandwiches for all of us. Jeremy takes our orders and calls Jersey Mike's, the sub place
next to my mom's shop. I start to tell Jeremy not to order
from them, remembering what a hard time they've been giving my mom about her expansion. But I can't think of anywhere else that will deliver and of the five of us, only Jan can
drive. And he refuses to leave us alone after last time.

"It's not that I don't trust you," he says. "It's me. I just
worry too much."

"Oh, I wouldn't trust us," Jillian says, winking at him. This
makes him smile and I feel a little jealous of how easy it is
for Jillian. She seems to know the exact thing to say to make
people happy. Even Jeremy. Even though she is constantly
deflecting any of his romantic overtures, he still keeps looking at her like she's pluperfect—more than perfect.

"Order extra bacon," Jan tells Jeremy before he hangs up
the phone. "So I hear you girls are going to this fancy shindig," Jan says, nodding at the boxes we're filling.

"Only if I can find someone to go with me," Claire says.
"I don't want to be the fifth wheel." I start to mention that
Jillian isn't exactly going *with* Charlie when Jeremy pipes up.

"I'll go," he says. Jillian looks over at him. I'm expecting some snarky remark from her, but she doesn't say anything.

"You know you'd be going with *me*?" Claire asks. Jeremy nods. Jillian is watching them, her mouth opening and closing like a fish. Claire looks at him for a moment. "Okay," she finally says. "Might as well." Might as well isn't exactly what I would hope for in response to an invitation, but Jeremy seems fine with it. I look over at Jillian, who is shaking her head. She seems surprised by this turn of events and a tiny bit perturbed. I can't help but wonder if she's a little jealous.

My cell phone hoots from my jacket pocket. I walk over to where I hung it on the hook near the back door. "Hello?" I say, turning away from where Claire and Jillian are having an intense discussion about what to wear to the Umlaut event. "Wait," I say, "I can't hear you." I step out the back door and into the alley, letting the door whoosh shut behind me.

"I asked if you need me to pick you up tomorrow," Charlie says. I pause, confused. "For the swim meet?" Charlie prompts.

"Are you sure it's okay to fraternize with the enemy?" I ask.

"Um, Piper, it's a swim meet, not war." There is a big crash in the background and then a series of thuds.

"Charlie?" I ask.

"I'm here," he says.

"Where are you?" I ask, surprised that he's out somewhere. He has this four point ritual that he performs before each meet. The first is sleep—at least eight hours. Two of the steps are food-related. Another involves ingesting as much coffee as humanly possible the morning of the meet.

"Listen, Pipe. I gotta go." There's more thudding, then a ripping sound.

"Charlie, is everything—"

"I'll be in front of your house at seven," Charlie says. The phone is dead before I can answer. I try to call him back, but it clicks immediately over to voice mail. I stare at my phone, not sure what to do. Part of me wants to find him—just to make sure he's okay. If I knew where Charlie was or what he was doing, I'd figure out a way to get there, but his phone is off and I have no idea where to even begin looking for him. I try his home phone, hoping to get Frank, but it just rings and rings. Right as I'm about to hang up and call my mom to ask her to go over there, Charlie's dad picks up.

"Hey, Mr. Wishman," I say. "It's Piper." He doesn't say anything. "From next door? I mean, I'm not next door right now . . ." I know I'm babbling, but I'm not sure exactly what to say.

"What can I do for you, Piper?" Charlie's dad asks. His voice sounds thick and I wonder if I woke him up. Instantly, I feel guilty for calling. Frank tends to sleep weird hours. Charlie is forever telling me to keep it down when I'm over there.

"Listen, I'm sorry to wake you, but I just talked to Charlie and—"

"Charlie's sleeping," he says, cutting me off.

"Oh," I say. "It was just that he got off the phone so quickly and I . . ." I trail off, unsure of what else to say. I start to congratulate him on the Umlaut thing, but he cuts me off again.

"If that's it—" he says.

"Yeah," I say. "Um, thanks and I'm sorry again—" But the phone is dead before I can finish. I look at the screen on my phone. *Charlie Home—Call ended.*

"Piper?" Jan pushes the back door open and looks at me. I slip my phone into my pocket and smile at him. "You okay?" he asks. I nod, but don't look at him. "You seem a little sad tonight."

"No," I say, "I'm good." I know Jan doesn't believe me. In addition to my cheeks turning bright red and my tic thingy in my left eye, it's the words that give me away. Whenever I say *I'm good*, it means I'm anything but good. Thankfully Jan doesn't say anything else. He just touches my shoulder briefly as I walk past him into the kitchen.

Jeremy is laughing so hard at something that he's having trouble breathing. Claire and Jillian are both staring at him with their arms folded. He finally calms down enough to speak. "Let me get this straight," he says. "You thought that by adding a bunch of herbs and spices and junk to some truffles, you could make people fall in love?" Jillian glares at him as he starts laughing again.

"You told him?" I ask. Claire nods toward Jillian, who manages to look slightly sheepish.

"It wasn't one of our best ideas," she admits.

Jeremy stares at the ceiling for a moment. "I think it's brilliant. There's just one major flaw," he says.

"Oh and what's that?" Jillian asks, her arms still folded.

"You were trying to make people fall in love, right?" Jillian nods impatiently. "I think that's where you went wrong. Your goal should have been to make people *think* they'd fallen in love."

"What's the difference?" Jillian asks.

It's Jeremy's turn to be impatient. "Symptoms of love are easy to measure and manipulate. Dilated pupils. Elevated heart rate. Flushed cheeks. If you can find ingredients that manufacture enough of those indicators, I think you could convince someone that he's in love."

"You mean trick someone," I say. Jeremy shrugs.

"But we wanted to make people *really* fall in love," Claire says.

"That's scientifically impossible," Jeremy says. "Even if you overlook the obvious confounding factors, there's no way to empirically prove the presence of something as nebulous as love." I look over at Jillian expecting her to say something, but she's just looking at Jeremy with this half smile on her face.

"What?" Jeremy asks, looking at her. She shrugs and starts folding more boxes. I am pretty sure this is the very first time I've ever seen Jillian at a loss for words.

chapter **twelve**

I hate to admit it, but this is good," I say, taking another bite of the bacon truffle. Jan had a batch of bacon truffles put together and chilling in the deep freeze as soon as the bacon arrived. He insisted we try one as soon as they were ready.

"Jeremy, that is some serious praise coming from a girl who doesn't like candy," Jan says. We've been taking turns eating our sandwiches and boxing up truffles.

"Another thing I hate to admit," I say, looking at my half-eaten veggie sub sitting on the desk, "is that Mike's can make a mean sandwich."

"Why do you hate to admit that?" Jan asks. I tell him about my mom and how Jersey Mike's is making her plans for expansion impossible.

"The only other option is if Artie's closes," I say, mentioning the shop on the other side of hers. Jan smirks at me. "And as much as I love my mom, the thought of a world without Artie's Pizza is too horrible to consider." This makes Claire laugh. I am a well-known Artie's junky. They even gave me one of their tie-dyed staff shirts last year for free.

Jillian looks up from where she's adding raspberries to the freshly made batch of truffle base. "It's not the best location for a high-end flower shop, wedged between a pizza parlor and a sandwich shop. She should relocate." I nod, remembering that I recently said almost the exact same thing to my mother.

"Speaking of expansions . . ." I say.

Jan sighs. He's been talking about knocking down the wall between his shop and the empty one next door ever since the bookstore moved down to the end of the strip. "Maybe when things slow down," he says. He's been saying that for months, and every time he does, I point out that things are doing the opposite of slowing down. Jan's is more popular all the time. "Maybe now that I have all this extra help," he says, smiling at us. Then his face gets serious. "Listen," he says. "I really do appreciate it."

"We know!" Jillian says, then laughs. It's the seventeenth time in the last hour that Jan has told us how much he appreciates our help. "You couldn't do this without us, blah, blah, blah."

"You're welcome," Claire says. "But it's no big deal. It's not like I had any other plans." She sounds a little wistful when she says it and I know she's thinking of how she used to spend every Friday night with Stuart. She looks over at me for a moment and I can see the sadness in her eyes.

"I didn't have anything else to do either," Jeremy says before taking a bite of his sandwich.

"Duh," Jillian says. I cringe a little, but Jeremy starts laughing.

I look at my watch. Almost eleven. "I've got to get home," I say. I called my mom earlier, telling her where I was. "I have to get some sleep or I'm going to be a mess at the meet tomorrow."

"Meet schmeet," Jillian says. "You should be much more worried about your date with Ben Donovan."

"You're going out with Ben Donovan?" Jeremy asks. His voice is incredulous.

"Is it so out of the realm of possibility?" I ask.

"Well yeah," Jeremy says, earning him three dirty looks, but he seems oblivious. "Why in the world would you want to go out with him?" Claire and Jillian both roll their eyes and look at me. I don't know what to say. I guess I'd never thought about it all that hard. I mean, Ben Donovan asks you out and you say yes, like Pavlov's dog and the ringing bell. It's just the automatic response.

"Because he's Ben Donovan," Claire says, voicing my thoughts.

Jeremy looks at me for a long moment. I can tell that reason doesn't float with him. "It's your heart," he says, lifting a tray of truffles and sliding them into the open refrigerator. I don't know what to say. It's as if the whole world just flipped. Here I am actually giving a second thought to what Jeremy Gardner thinks about me going out with Ben Donovan. I shake my head, forgetting that I'm still wearing the blinking hearts headband. They start clacking together like mad, making everyone laugh.

"Okay," Jan says, clapping his hands together. "This can all wait until tomorrow. Let's get you kiddos home before your parents wonder if I've spirited you all away."

"But what about . . ." I gesture to the empty boxes meant to hold truffles and the ones for the Consternation Hearts. They still need to be filled.

"Tomorrow," Jan says, attempting to herd us toward the door and his car that's parked out back.

"But I have the meet and then . . ." I trail off, not wanting to talk about Ben Donovan again. At least not in front of Jeremy. Jillian and Claire are also busy, Jillian with some family thing that she won't elaborate on and Claire at my mom's shop.

"I'll be here," Jeremy says. "I don't have anything to do."

"Again. Duh," Jillian says. This time we all laugh.

"I can't believe your car is a hearse," Jillian says as we all pile into Jan's car. I notice that Jeremy works it so he's right next to Jillian. Jan just laughs. He told me once that he bought it from a funeral home that was closing down, and that it's perfect for hauling big candy orders. He's right; you can just slide the boxes into the back along the rails mounted there. Creepy, but true.

Jan drops me off first. As I climb out, Claire and Jillian extract a promise that I will call them *immediately* after my date. Jeremy rolls his eyes. I wave as they pull away from the curb. I turn and start toward my house, where my mother has left the front porch light on. I look up at Charlie's window. I can't shake the feeling that there is something Charlie isn't telling me, something that he's hiding. I sigh and look away from his darkened window and walk inside. I peek in my mom's room and whisper good night. The light from the hall falls across her face. She smiles at me, but doesn't open her eyes.

I don't bother showering, reasoning that in less than eight hours I'll be in the pool. I lie awake staring at my ceiling, trying to force myself to sleep. But even when I finally start to drift off, I'm still listening for the loud thump above me that never comes.

It feels like I've only been asleep for five minutes when my alarm rings. I'm still half asleep as I pull on my suit, then my warm-ups, and heft my bag from where I left it by the door. Charlie is just backing his car out when I walk outside. I climb into the passenger side, resisting the urge to lie down in the backseat and get some more sleep. I don't tell Charlie what I'm doing after the meet, just that I don't need a ride home. He nods, not taking his eyes off the road. He doesn't say anything on the whole ride over to the pool. He's still silent as we walk into the Natatorium. We enter the building and he turns toward the guys' locker room.

I grab the sleeve of his sweatshirt. "Charlie," I say. He looks at my hand on his arm, like he's not sure how it got there, then at my face. "I want—" I pause, seeing the look in his eyes. He's standing right there only a couple of feet from me, but the look in his eyes is far away.

"What is it, Piper?" he asks. His voice is flat.

"I just wanted—" Charlie keeps looking at me and as he does I can kind of see him in there. Kind of see the Charlie I know.

"Hey, Wishman!" A guy yells from the other end of the hallway. "Get your butt in the pool."

Charlie doesn't turn, just keeps looking at me. "I just wanted to say good luck," I say finally.

"You too," he says. He smiles slightly and then turns to walk away, but not before I see the look in his eyes. He's pulled back again. I start to call out to him, to ask him something, anything. To ask him where he is and how can I get there? But he's walking into the locker room and before I can say anything the door whooshes closed behind him and he's gone.

The good thing about going out with Ben Donovan right after the swim meet is, I'm so nervous about not making a fool of myself in the pool that I don't have time to be nervous about our date. On the downside, the news of our date has gotten around to everyone on the swim team. I feel like in addition to being slightly freaked at the notion of actually being alone with Ben Donovan, there's extra pressure for me to be smart and funny and beautiful. Otherwise, everyone is going to assume that Ben Donovan was suffering from temporary insanity when he asked me out and therefore cannot be held responsible for his poor judgment. Girls I barely know keep coming up to me in the locker room and telling me good luck. A few of them are excited, like maybe I'm some kind of hero, but mostly they seem sort of scared for me. Those girls freak me out—it's like they are whispering good luck with my upcoming open-heart surgery.

The pool deck is a madhouse like it always is during meets. The Natatorium has four competition pools. It's huge—part of the Olympic complex. Since it's so much better than any of the pools the city schools have, or even the private schools, all the teams within driving distance have all of their meets here. Charlie likes to tease me about how my team's slumming it when we compete against the public schools.

I step out onto the deck. I'm always surprised at how big everything is. Rows of empty seats climb up toward the ceiling on all sides, making me feel like I'm in the middle of a huge bowl. I drop my bag on one of the benches and slip out of my sweats. Jillian made me promise that I would not under any circumstance wear anything made out of sweatshirt material on my date. Even I could figure that one out. I assured her that I would wear something nice. She wanted specifics. I described my outfit: a pair of my nicer jeans, a long-sleeved thermal with rhinestone buttons, and my purple flats. I pull my swim cap on and shove my hair up into it. I adjust my goggles, pushing them hard into my eye sockets to make sure they won't leak.

"Hey, Paisley!" I turn and see Peter waving at me from the water a couple of lanes away. He hangs from the diving block and makes monkey noises. Several girls around me laugh. I just shake my head. It hasn't gotten any funnier after the three hundredth time. Another swimmer pulls up next to him and yanks him down. Peter says something to him and he turns my way. I feel a flutter in my stomach as he smiles at me. Ben Donovan. *Well, Jeremy,* I think as I prepare to dive in. *There's your answer.* But all through my warm-up, I can't shake the question that floats through my brain. That flutter. Is that enough? Is that all there is?

Artie's is packed when we get there. The line to order snakes away from the counter and out the door.

"Why don't you see if you can find us a table and I'll order," Ben Donovan tells me. I start over to where I see one of the Artie's workers wiping down a booth. "Piper!" I turn around. "What do you like on your pizza?" I tell him anything except olives. Olives freak me out. They look like eyeballs and taste like fish. Yuck. Someone snags the booth I was heading toward, but I grab a table near the front window when it's free.

A boy, not much older than Dom, keeps feeding quarters into the claw machine behind me. He's on his last quarter and still hasn't won anything. I decide to tell him the trick that Charlie figured out.

"If you wait until the claw stops swinging, you'll have a better chance of getting that dog," I say. The boy looks over at me, trying to figure out if I'm just messing with him. "Seriously," I say, standing up and walking over behind him. "Better yet, go for that bear." I point to a brown bear with a propeller hat near the back. "The ones that are lying down are easier to pick up." The boy nods and feeds his last quarter into the slot and starts the claw moving toward the back. "That's it," I say, leaning around to look in the side window. "A little more." He taps the joystick. "Perfect," I say. "Now, you wait." The timer above the claw counts down slowly.

The boy is getting antsy, but he doesn't push the button to lower the claw. I'm hoping Charlie's techniques will work. They don't always, but I have a shelf full of cheap stuffed animals to prove that they do more often than not. The claw drops and slowly lowers around the bear and lifts it.

"Woo!" the boy yells. He reaches into the trap door and pulls out the stuffed bear. "Thanks," he says to me. I smile as he starts toward the back of Artie's with the bear held high over his head. I sit back down at our table just as Ben Donovan finishes ordering and starts making his way over to where I'm sitting. The boy with the bear nearly collides with him as he races past.

"Hey," Ben Donovan says, sitting down across from me. "It's busy," he says, stating the obvious. I nod, agreeing to the obvious. "Those things are a scam," he says, nodding to the claw machine. "I never win." I think about telling him Charlie's techniques, but someone calls his name from the order line. I look up and spot Peter and Sarah, standing waiting to order.

Peter presses something into Sarah's hand and walks over to us. He pulls a chair out, flips it around, and sits so he's riding it like a horse. "Can we join you?" he asks. It's not really a question, but I say sure anyway. Secretly I'm grateful. I know Peter will dominate the conversation as he always does. Which in this case is a good thing. Even though Ben Donovan and I have been together less than half an hour, we've already run out of things to talk about, having covered the usual: swimming, school, Montrose gossip, and even the Braves' prospects for this year. I introduced that last topic, showing how desperate I was.

Sarah joins us a few minutes later. She hands Peter some change. I shake my head. I guess she should be glad that in addition to making her wait in line, he didn't make her pay. Artie delivers our pizzas to our table himself. He barely has time to say hello before someone in the kitchen starts yelling his name. He waves and hurries back to the kitchen, where I can see the orders stacked up two and three deep on the clips.

"That Wishman is a machine," Ben Donovan says, taking a slice of pizza. I nod. He's right. Charlie won every event he swam, even the 800 IM, which he entered at the last minute because one of his teammates cramped up during the thousand and had to drop out.

"With him swimming against us, we don't stand a chance at state this year," Peter says, already making short work of his second piece of pizza. "I say we take him out."

"On a date?" Sarah asks, confused. I make big eyes at Peter, but he just laughs.

"No, you know, as in whack him." Sarah still seems confused so I help out.

"Apparently, Peter is aware that the only way he has a chance to beat Charlie Wishman is if he puts Charlie out of commission." I turn to Peter. "Is that right?"

"Exactly," Peter says. He takes a drink of his soda. "I've got it," he says. "You're friends with him, right, Paisley?" I nod slowly, wondering where this is going. "What if you put something in some of those truffles you make? You know, something that alters him in some way." I feel my cheeks flush.

"Piper would never do that," Ben Donovan says, glancing over at me.

"How would you know?" Peter asks, rolling his eyes. I look over at him too, wondering how exactly he would know what I would or wouldn't do.

Ben Donovan shrugs. "Just a feeling," he says. He smiles at me and I can't help but smile back.

I look over at Sarah, who seems content to nibble on her one piece of pizza and just listen to the guys talk about every minute detail of the meet. When Peter starts analyzing Charlie's flip turn, I decide to make a break for it. "Listen, my mom's shop is right next door," I say, standing up. "Thank you for lunch." Ben Donovan stands up and pushes his chair in.

"You sure?" he asks. I nod and smile. He takes my arm and walks me out onto the sidewalk. "Listen, Piper. I'm sorry. I didn't know Peter was going to show up and—"

"It's fine," I say. "I had fun." I feel a fluttery feeling in my stomach, but I can't tell if it's because I'm not exactly being truthful or because Ben Donovan is holding my hand.

"Really?" he asks. I nod. "Well maybe we could go out again sometime?" he asks.

"Oh!" I say. "I almost forgot." And Jillian would *kill* me if I had. I tell him about the Umlaut event. I start to apologize for the lameness of it, but he smiles.

"Sounds fun," he says. He leans toward me and brushes my cheek with his, like he was going to kiss me, but changed his mind at the last minute. He pulls back when the door opens behind us and Peter and Sarah walk out.

"Whoops. Sorry," Peter says in an anything but an apologetic tone. I smile and shake my head at him.

"Thanks again," I say. I turn to walk down the sidewalk to my mom's shop. Before I reach the door, I hear my name behind me.

"Piper!" Ben Donovan calls from where he's unlocking his car. "I'll call you tonight." I smile and wave. My cheeks start burning. I feel like everyone on the sidewalk is looking at me. I pull the door of my mom's shop open, pausing a moment before going in, trying to figure out how I feel about that. *I'm the girl who Ben Donovan is going to call tonight.* I don't have long to think about it before Claire and Jillian spill out of the back of the shop, demanding details. My mom follows them, drying her hands on a towel.

"Did you have fun?" she asks.

I shrug. "It was good," I say.

"Just good?" Jillian shrieks. "You just went out with Ben Donovan. How can a date with Ben Donovan be just *good?*"

"Okay," I say. "It was great. Stupendous. Awesome." Jillian seems pleased by this response. But saying it out loud only makes it clearer that it's not the truth. Being with Ben Donovan was good. Saying anything else is a lie.

"I was going to have you order pizza for dinner tonight," Mom says. "But I guess you just had pizza."

"Oh, don't let that stop you," I say. "I can always eat pizza." Mom smiles and goes into the back. She returns with her wallet and hands it to me.

"If you girls are coming over, get enough for everyone," Mom says to Jillian and Claire. They both call home on the way over to Artie's. Jillian tells me her mom is just happy to have her out of her hair for the evening.

"She gets majorly stressed about these events," she says.

"Just about anything can set her off. Last night she freaked when she realized we were out of milk."

Claire has to plead with her mother to let her come over. She sighs when she hangs up the phone. "She said she misses me." Claire rolls her eyes.

"Would you rather she didn't?" I ask.

"No, but I'd rather she tell me the truth. She doesn't miss me. She misses having free childcare so she can go play tennis."

I smirk at her. "Now who's cynical?" Claire swats at my arm, making me smile. It's so great to see the real Claire. I was starting to wonder if she was permanently gone. Even before Stuart officially broke it off with her, that relationship was stealing something from her. Some of her light, I guess. Seeing her smile and joke with me and Jillian makes me remember how she used to be.

While we wait in line, we try to decide what we want to order. I vote for veggie. Jillian wants Hawaiian.

"How come Hawaii is the only state with an official pizza?" Jillian asks. "Why not Georgia?"

"Because no one wants to eat peanut and peach pizza," I say, making Claire laugh.

We agree on two large pizzas, one half veggie, half Hawaiian, the other plain cheese. I step up to the counter and accept the ribbing from the owner that I knew was coming.

"We should rename this place Piper's," Artie says.

"Would I get free pizza?" I ask.

Artie laughs. "That would probably put me out of business."

"It might," I say. I give him our order, telling him we'll pick it up at six when my mom's shop closes. He hands it off to one of the guys working the ovens. I start to walk over to where Jillian and Claire are playing the claw machine, but Artie stops me.

"So, do you want to just take your other order with you when you come get these?" he asks.

"What other order?" I ask.

Artie walks over to a long metal strip that they hang their orders on. He pulls a slip down and reads from it. "One heart-shaped Vegetarian's Delight," he says. "Absolutely no olives." He looks up at me. "I've never done a heart-shaped pizza before, but it's a great idea. I might steal it."

"I didn't order that," I say.

Artie shrugs. "Well, someone did. It's all paid for." He looks at the order slip. I look over to where Claire is pulling a red and white monkey out of the prize door. She holds it up toward me and smiles. She was also a member of Charlie's Brotherhood of the Claw. He named it that, saying it sounded mysterious.

"I guess we'll just pick it up with the others," I tell Artie. "Thanks."

"No problem," Artie says, relaying the message to one of the guys making the pizzas. I walk over to where Jillian is trying her hand at the claw.

"Dang," she says when the pink dog she managed to pick up drops before it reaches the chute.

"So guess what?" I ask.

"What?" Jillian asks, feeding another quarter into the machine. I tell them about the heart-shaped pizza. Jillian forgets the claw, still hanging over the pile of stuffed animals. She puts her hands over her heart. "That is one of the most romantic things I have ever heard." Then she looks at me with big eyes. "It has to be Ben Donovan," she says.

"Maybe," I say.

"Who else could it be?" Jillian asks. I raise one eyebrow. "I don't mean it like that. I mean, it *could* be anyone. My money's on Ben Donovan."

"It has to be him," Claire says.

"Maybe," I say again, but I just can't picture Ben Donovan going to all that trouble. The more I know of him, the more I'm convinced that very little concerns Ben Donovan outside of Ben Donovan. "Maybe it was you," I say, narrowing my eyes at Jillian.

Jillian rolls her eyes. "What evidence do you have of that?"

"Well, you have been leaving all that stuff in my locker," I say.

"Nail polish, fig-colored Burt's Bees, and that cute clip with cherries on it?"

"And the banana and the peanut butter and the pin and the cockroach," I say, ticking them off on my fingers. I watch the claw drop behind Jillian and retract, a pink snake clutched in its grip. Jillian starts looking wildly at the floor around us. "What are you doing?" I ask her.

"I'm looking for your marbles. The ones you've obviously lost." I look over at Claire who is smiling and shaking her head.

"Jillian, have you or have you not been leaving paper bags with gifts in them in my locker?"

"What are you talking about?" Jillian says. The claw drops the snake down the chute. "I haven't left anything in your locker in paper bags."

I look at her, trying to figure out if she's lying. She's not. She seems genuinely baffled by my questions. I tell Claire and Jillian about the gifts. Claire smiles and Jillian actually starts bouncing on the balls of her feet.

"It has to be someone with access to your locker," Jillian says. I reach around her, grab the snake and hand it to her. She smiles at it. "So romantic." I shake my head.

"All three of those people who can get in my locker are right here," I say. Jillian frowns for a moment, thinking. Then she smiles at me. "The only thing better than a Valentine is a *secret* Valentine," she says. I roll my eyes. I'm pretty sure if I told Jillian someone was leaving rolls of toilet paper and bags of ABC gum in my locker she'd find it romantic.

I wave at Artie as we leave, telling him we'll be back to pick up the pizzas in a few hours. We spend the rest of the afternoon helping my mom organize the coolers and pulling the wilted stock from the bins to make room for the big shipment arriving in a few days. We wear flannel shirts and fleece coats that my mom keeps for working in the cooler, though really I don't mind the cold. The best part is the noise of the fans as they crank out cold air. It makes talking nearly impossible, so Jillian can't continue her nonstop chatter about my secret Valentine.

"Let's call it a day," Mom says from the doorway. We step back into the workroom, shedding our coats and hats. Jillian's lips are slightly blue and Claire's teeth are chattering. My fingers feel numb. "If you'll go pick up dinner, I'll pull the car around." The three of us walk back over to Artie's.

"Order up!" Artie yells when he sees us. The three of us crowd the counter to take a look at the heart-shaped pizza.

"Ooh," Jillian squeals. "This is so cool." I can feel my cheeks get pink. Claire is smiling too.

"It's great," I say to Artie.

"Was it a guy who called?" Jillian asks him.

Artie holds up his hand. "That is strictly on a need-to-know basis," he says.

"We need to know," Claire says.

"No, you *want* to know," Artie says. "And I'm not going to spill the beans." He winks at me as he closes the box. "Whoever it is sure knows you," he says. I nod and thank him for the pizza. As we walk to the car, I try to figure that one out. A lot of people sort of know me, but *know* me? I don't think anyone really does.

chapter **thirteen**

The second we pull into the driveway, Jillian is out of the car. She walks directly over to Charlie's. She was asking questions about him during the whole drive home. I caught my mother looking at me in the rearview mirror, one eyebrow raised. Jillian insisted we invite Charlie over for pizza "because well, after the meet, I'm sure he's starving." Claire and I both pointed out that the meet was over six hours ago, giving Charlie plenty of time to eat enough food to feed a small country, but she just waved the back of her hand at us as she hopped the flower bed separating our front lawn from the Wishmans'.

Claire and I help Mom carry the pizzas and the flowers in-side. She brought the flowers for Mrs. Bateman. Apparently when Mom called a couple of hours ago "just to see how things were going," Dom and Lucy had barricaded themselves at the top of the playscape in the backyard and were pelting Mrs. Bateman with toys whenever she came near.

"Thank you so much," Mom says, handing Mrs. Bateman the flowers and what I'm sure is a sizeable check. She walks her out while I slide the pizzas onto the counter.

Claire pulls a stack of plastic plates out of one of the cabinets. "It is so much fun working with your mom," she says. "She knows so much about flowers. Did you know that if you put an aspirin in the water before you add the flowers, they'll last longer?" I nod. "And if you want them to bloom faster, you just put an apple near them?" She pauses and smiles. "Thanks for suggesting it," she says.

"It seems to be good for you."

She nods. "I think it's good for your mom too," she says. I wait for her to explain, but she just gives me the same Cheshire Cat grin Jillian's been giving me for days. She turns, leans against the counter, and looks at me. "Tell me the truth."

"About what?" I ask. I open the fridge to pull out juice, milk, and lemonade.

"Pipe, I've known you for seven years. I know when you're lying. How was your date with Ben Donovan really?"

I sigh and look at her. "I don't know. I mean, it was fine."

"Fine and good," Claire says.

"We just didn't have that much to say to each other."

"You seem surprised by that," she says. "What did you expect?"

"I don't know. Something," I say. "I mean he is Ben Donovan."

Claire snorts, a habit she picked up from me. "Piper, you're smarter than that."

I nod. "Yeah," I say. "I guess I'm not really his type."

"No," she says. "I'm not entirely sure he's *your* type."

"I don't think I have a type," I say. "I'm not that great at relationships."

"You want to know what I think?" Claire asks.

"I'm not sure," I say. "Whenever people say that, they're about to tell you something bad."

"Not bad, just true," she says.

I put the carton of milk, the bottle of lemonade, and the bottle of apple juice on the counter. "Okay," I say. I take a deep breath. "I'm ready."

Claire laughs. "I think you like to sabotage yourself."

"What are you talking about?" I ask.

"The few times you've gone out with a guy, you do a preemptive strike so you can make sure you get away before he gets too close."

"I don't do that," I say. Claire just looks at me. "When?"

"Casey was too short. Eric's voice was too 'adenoidal.' Peter didn't say the word robot correctly." She ticks them off on her fingers as she lists them.

"But all those things are true," I say. "Casey Williams is like five feet tall."

"He was thirteen," Claire says. I wave my hand, dismissing her point.

"Eric constantly had to clear his throat and well, the robot thing was sort of minor, but it was just a symptom of Peter's larger problem which is that he's completely intolerable. And seriously. Have you even considered what it would be like if I dated Peter? I mean, Peter Piper?" This makes Claire laugh.

"Maybe," she says. I frown at her, but before she can say anything else, the front door opens and Mom comes in, followed by Jillian and Charlie and the terrible twosome.

"Go wash up," Mom tells Dom and Lucy. They race up the stairs. "Use soap!" Mom yells. "I better go supervise," she says to me, smiling.

"Charlie was hungry," Jillian says.

"Charlie, have you ever not been hungry?" I ask.

"No," he says without having to think about it. "I'm pretty much always hungry. What are we having?" I nod toward the stack of pizza boxes at the end of the counter. "Awesome. I love Artie's."

Jillian tugs Charlie's sleeve, pulling him toward the stack of boxes. She flips the top one open. "Look," she says. "It's a heart."

"I can see that," Charlie says, peering into the box. "But *why* is it a heart?"

"Piper has a secret Valentine," Jillian says. I swear she actually swoons a little when she says it. "Isn't that romantic?"

Charlie pulls one of the pieces from the box and takes a bite out of it. "It's tasty," he says. Jillian rolls her eyes in my direction. Footsteps thud all the way down the stairs. Dom tears around the corner followed closely by Lucy.

161

"I want to sit by Charlie!" Lucy yells, grabbing his free hand. She pulls him over to the table. Jillian is quick to claim the chair on the other side of Charlie, sliding it closer to him as she sits down. I grab the cups and plates and forks. Claire brings the stack of pizza boxes over and places them in the middle of the table.

"I'll help," Charlie says, starting to get up, but Lucy pushes him back down and climbs into his lap. I smirk, thinking Jillian is just an older and only slightly more subtle version of my little sister.

Mom comes down the stairs. Her hair is up in a ponytail and she's changed into jeans and a T-shirt. My mother is really pretty. She has the same brown hair as me, but hers is run through with gold. And where my eyes are sort of a milky blue, like sea glass, hers are such a dark shade of blue that they almost seem purple in certain light. She comes up to me and puts her arm around my waist.

"This is nice," she says.

"Just a quiet dinner at the Paisley house," I say. She laughs as we watch Claire dishing out slices of pizza to Dom and Lucy. Dom flips his backwards and starts eating the crust first. Lucy barely touches hers. She's too busy making sure Jillian knows Charlie is with *her*.

"You're *my* Valentine, right, Charlie?" Lucy asks, glaring at Jillian.

"Stop pestering him," my mother says. She walks over and lifts Lucy out of his lap and slides her into her own chair.

I follow and sit in the last empty chair, between my mother and Claire.

"Who's your Valentine?" Jillian asks Dom.

He squints at her. "Valentine's Day is stupid," he says.

"Mommy! Dom said a bad word," Lucy says around a mouthful of pizza.

"But that's what Piper said," Dom says. It's suddenly quiet and everyone looks at me.

"I didn't say that," I argue, but I'm not that sure.

"You did too," Dom says. His eyes start filling up with tears.

"Maybe you're right," I say softly. I put my slice of pizza back on my plate. Suddenly I don't feel much like eating. It's one thing to be cynical when you're my age, but when you're five? "Dom," I say. "Maybe I was wrong. Maybe I was just being grouchy."

He looks at me for a moment, then smiles. "You are pretty grouchy," he says, making everyone laugh.

"Not all the time!" I say.

"Just when you wake up," Claire says.

"And when you're hungry," Charlie points out.

"And when you're doing homework," Lucy adds.

"When you're tired," Mom says.

"Or sick," Charlie says.

"Or hot," Jillian says.

"Or cold," Dom says.

"Okay, okay," I say, holding up my hands. "But only then."

"But that's *all the time*," Lucy says. This makes everyone laugh again. My cell phone goes off. It sounds like a herd of cows.

"Saved by the moo," I say, pushing away from the table. I look over at Charlie, who just smiles. I have yet to see him fiddling with my phone. I pick it up and look at the screen before putting it to my ear. "Hey, Jan," I say.

"Guess who I just got off the phone with?" Jan asks.

"Umm . . ." I look at the ceiling.

"Forget it," Jan says. "You're a lousy guesser. I just got off the phone with the Food Network."

"Cool," I say, mostly because I don't know what else to say.

"They want to film a segment *here!*" he says.

"Wow," I say. "That's amazing. You must be psyched."

"No, Piper, you don't understand," Jan says. "They're going to be here in two days."

"That's soon," I say, stating the obvious. Everyone at the table is quiet and looking at me. I smile at them, then stare back down at the floor and listen.

"I need to stock the cases and clean the windows and clear the tables so they'll have room for the cameras and—" Jan keeps listing all the things that need to happen.

"We'll help," I say. I look over at everyone sitting at the table. They all nod, making me smile. They don't even need to know what they are signing up for. They're in.

"That would be great, Piper. But listen, school comes first. I want you to make sure—"

"Jan," I say. "I'm good. Remember, I'm the queen of organization."

"She's the queen of grouchy too!" Dom yells.

Jan starts laughing. "Okay, Queen Grouchy. Whatever time you and your cohorts can spare would be much appreciated."

"I'll see you tomorrow," I say. I click off and put down the phone. I take a deep breath.

"Well, tell us!" Jillian says. I laugh. Patient, she is not. I tell them all about the Food Network coming and Jan freaking. "So do we get to be on television?" Jillian asks. I shrug.

"Whatever we can do to help," my mother says.

"Mom," I say. "You're busy too."

"I know," she says, standing up. "But I know you'd all help me if I needed it." She picks up two of the empty pizza boxes and walks with them into the kitchen.

"He asked if we could be there tomorrow," I say to Jillian, who nods. "And Claire, if you want to—"

"Of course. Once I finish sorting the ribbon and restocking the gift cards and dusting the vases." I smile. She clearly loves working for my mom.

"What about me?" Charlie asks. "I'm not so sure I can make candy, but I'm not totally worthless."

"No," Jillian says. "You're not." Lucy gives her a dirty look.

"I didn't know if you'd want to," I say.

"Count me in," he says. "Maybe there'll be some irregulars that need eating."

"I'll help," Lucy says.

"Me too!" Dom says, not wanting to be left out.

"The best way you two can help is to get changed into your pajamas," my mom says. Both Dom and Lucy start to protest, but Mom just points to the stairs. They slide out of their seats and head for their rooms. "I'll be up to tuck you in in a few minutes."

"Can Charlie do it?" Lucy asks.

"No, I'm sure Charlie—"

"I don't mind," Charlie says. "I'm pretty decent at the bedtime stories."

"I want a scary one," Dom says.

"One with princesses," Lucy says.

"Scary princess story," Charlie says. "Got it."

"I'll help," Jillian says, smiling up at Charlie.

He shrugs. "As long as you're willing to do the voices." He pushes away from the table to follow Dom and Lucy.

"The what?" Jillian asks, following him to the stairs. Claire and I laugh. We've heard Charlie's stories before. Every character has a different voice. Jillian is in for a treat.

Claire and I help Mom clean up the kitchen. I listen as they talk about blooming times and which greenery goes better with which flowers. I scrape the plates and start loading the dishwasher. I look at Claire as my mom talks, and see her smiling. She definitely seems better. I haven't heard her even mention Stuart's name in a couple of days. My mother walks over to her calendar. Even though Claire does it quickly, I see her sneak a look at her phone. She frowns at it before sliding it back into her pocket. She looks over at me, but I pretend that I'm intent on cleaning off a stray bit of cheese from one of the plates. I guess even when people seem like they're fine, they might not be. They're just pretending. I wonder if everyone is. If everyone's heart is broken to some degree. I look into the sink, still full of suds from washing the dishes. I trace a heart in the bubbles and then without even thinking about it, I draw a jagged line right down the middle. I hear a horse whinny from upstairs and then the sounds of a princess with a very strong New York accent talking about her knight in shining armor. I listen as my mother and Claire discuss their strategy for Valentine's Day. I smile as I wash the bubbles down the drain. Things are good. Not great. Not perfect, but good.

chapter fourteen

Jan's shop looks like a bomb went off in it. Everything has been taken off the shelves and pulled away from the walls so we can clean. I'm standing on a stool behind the counter and handing big jars of jawbreakers and rock candy down to Jillian.

"How many is that?" Jeremy asks from the other side of the counter.

Charlie tries to answer, but it just comes out sounding something like "Elve." He gives up and uses his fingers, holding up both hands then two fingers.

"Twelve," Jillian says, as if the rest of us are mathematically impaired. Charlie pushes another marshmallow in his mouth, wedging it inside his right cheek. He closes his eyes for a moment then shakes his head. He goes into the back and thankfully lets the door bump shut behind him. He comes out after a moment, wiping his mouth with a paper towel.

"You win," he says to Jeremy, who is grinning like mad. Jeremy managed to wedge thirteen marshmallows into his mouth before calling it quits.

"Finally," Jeremy says. "The great Charlie Wishman goes down." Charlie shakes his head and smiles. Jeremy laughs and rubs his hands together. "I spent five years getting lapped by you. Finally vengeance is mine." He pushes back through the door into the kitchen, where Jan is standing over the stove, stirring pots of chocolate. We hear him announce his win to Jan, then Jan laughing.

Jillian, Jeremy, and I have been here since right after breakfast. When Charlie showed up, I introduced him to Jeremy, who shook his hand very seriously. They managed to get out a couple of fake how-do-you-dos before they both started laughing. Charlie said they used to swim together. Jeremy amended that.

"Charlie is a swimmer. What I do is more like sustained non-drowning."

"Come on," Charlie said. "You weren't that bad." Jeremy just looked at him.

Charlie started to argue, but finally smiled and nodded. "Um. You did your best?" Charlie said, smirking.

Jeremy laughed. "That's exactly what Coach said just before he cut me from the team." This made Charlie smile. After that it seemed like every sentence they uttered for

the next hour started with: "Hey, remember that time—"
Following the hundredth swim team / Boy Scouts / Little
League walk down memory lane, I tuned them out. There's
only so much guy bonding I can take.

Jan put Jillian and me in charge of the front of the shop,
while he enlisted Jeremy to help in the kitchen. At first I
was a little put out that Jeremy got to work in the kitchen,
but Jan explained that he was working on a surprise and
didn't want me to see it until it was finished. Jillian and I
have been dusting and wiping and arranging and throwing out for nearly five hours. If this were my mom's shop,
we would have been done hours ago. Her style is very
minimalist. Less is more. Jan's style is, as Jillian says, "Early
Pack Rat." Every spare bit of wall space is covered with re-
claimed street signs and vintage metal plaques advertising
everything from seltzer water to motor oil. He has dozens
of old tin toys lined up on a shelf above the menu board.
One of his old surfboards is suspended from the ceiling
above the taffy and caramel bins. He's hung all of his old
rock climbing equipment from hooks over the barrels of
hard candies.

So far we've managed to dust everything and wipe down
every flat surface. For the last hour, before we were inter-
rupted by the World Marshmallow Championships, we've
been hauling bags of hard candy from the back storeroom
and filling all of the barrels. They're almost spilling over.

Having Jillian around does keep things interesting. So far

she's asked me to tell her, in detail, everything I can remember about my very brief conversation with Ben Donovan. He called last night right after Jillian, Claire, and Charlie had left. He had to make it fast because his dad was having him go to some dinner party. I was wiped out and half asleep as he was talking, but he didn't seem to mind that I had little to say.

"Did you ask him about the gifts in your locker?" Jillian asks. I shake my head. "What about the balloons at your house?" she presses, referring to the ones that were tied to my front door sometime Friday night. I hadn't even noticed them when I stumbled out of the house on my way to the meet.

I shake my head again. "I really don't think it's him," I say.

"It has to be him," she says, as if that settles it. I pour the bag of star mints into the bin, watching them tumble over each other.

"You like him though, right?" Jillian says.

"He's nice," I say, and it's true, but he's nice sort of like yogurt is nice or a brand-new pencil is nice.

"That's good," Jillian says, sounding distracted. She's watching Charlie fill one of the big apothecary jars on the counter with silver M&M's. Jan has them in any color you can imagine. Hot pink is the most popular followed by baby pink, purple, lavender, and silver. I always feel sort of bad for the brown ones. No one ever wants them.

"So what's left?" Charlie asks when he's finished refilling all of the jars.

I look around at the shop. "We need to clear some of the tables out to make room for the cameras and then someone needs to fix the Valentine's display." We all look over at the front window, which Jan has decorated for the upcoming holiday. It looks bad. Nearly all of the candy is gone and even cupid, who used to float serenely in the window, looks like he's taken a beating. Jan said a busload of tourists hit the shop late yesterday, cleaning him out of just about everything.

"I'll do the tables," Charlie says.

"I'll help," Jillian offers. She makes big eyes at me before walking over to where Charlie is already lifting one of the tables and carrying it toward the back. If Jeremy noticed any difference in Jillian since Charlie arrived, he hasn't given any indication of it. I'm pretty sure you'd have to be blind not to notice though. If Jillian says one more thing about Charlie's muscles, his hair, his shirt, his voice, or his eyes, I may just have to see how many marshmallows I can cram into *her* mouth.

My phone moos at me from my back pocket. I might have to ask Charlie to change it this time. I read the text from Claire.

There in 10
—C

I push my phone back in my pocket and look around. There's still so much to do, but Mom made me promise to finish early tonight. I have a big week in front of me with swim practice and school and the Food Network visit and the Umlaut thing. Mom said she wants me home "at a decent hour."

I start working on the Valentine's display. I fix cupid's wings so that he hangs straight again. I fluff the pink clouds hanging in the window. Yes, they are real cotton candy. Jan does nothing halfway. I restock all the candy, making sure there are plenty of Consternation Hearts. They're selling really well. Jan ordered another container of boxes and those are already half gone. I notice the jar of Jan's Fortune Hearts is nearly empty too. I walk toward the kitchen to retrieve more from the walk-in. I try to push the door open, but it's blocked.

"Wait!" Jan says. I wait. And wait.

"Jan, I have to—"

"Okay," he says. "Come in." I push the door open. Everyone is huddled around the island. I lean over Jillian's shoulder to see what they're all looking at.

"Ta-da," Jan says.

"It's a ring pop," I say, seeing the band of plastic supporting the oversized hunk of jewel-shaped candy.

"Not just any ring pop," Jan says. "Look." He holds one out to me. I take it and look at it. "Put it on," Jan says. I slide it onto my finger. Immediately it lights up, making the gem glow.

"Cool," I say.

"Wait for it," Jan says. I watch the ring as it starts to shift from the clear gem I put on my finger to a light pink color. Jeremy clicks the lights off, pitching the kitchen into darkness. The rings are the only lights in the room. I can see Jeremy's green one bobbing near the back door and Charlie's and Jillian's matching orange ones near the stove, and then a purple one appears where Jan is standing. Jeremy flips the lights back on. Even though they were only off for a moment, the sudden light is too bright in my eyes, making me squint. "These are cool, Jan," I say, studying mine again.

"Cool?" Jeremy asks, as if I just called them stupid.

"Um, supercool?" I say.

"These could revolutionize the confectionary industry." I raise my eyebrows, but Jan just smiles.

"They're cool, but how are colored ring pops going to revolutionize anything? Even if they do light up?" I ask.

"They're not just colored. They're mood ring pops," Jeremy says.

I look at my ring again, which is slowly shifting to blue. "So what do all the colors mean?" I ask.

"Well, that's the tricky part," Jeremy says. "We need to test them." He grabs a pad of paper from the desk and looks at Jillian.

"Describe your mood."

"Happy. I guess." Jeremy writes that on the pad and looks at Charlie.

"Happy," he says, but already his ring is changing to yellow. "Sort of."

"Sort of happy," Jeremy says, writing that down.

"This doesn't seem very scientific," I say.

Jeremy points at Jan. "Stressed," he says. We all look at his ring, which is careening past purple and headed toward black.

"Piper," Jeremy says. My ring keeps shifting from pink to purple to green and back again. "Confused," Jeremy says, writing that down. I frown at him.

"And I'm . . ." He tilts his head to one side and looks up at the ceiling. "Focused." I snort, but luckily a herd of cows starts making a racket from my pocket, keeping me from saying anything I might regret.

I look at my phone. Another text from Claire: **HELLO?**

I hear the knocking at the front door. "It's my mom," I say, slipping my ring off and laying it on the counter. I walk to the front and let her and Claire in. They are each carrying a huge flower arrangement. One is all roses: pink and red and orange and white. The other is a huge arrangement of tulips and gerbera daisies.

"Wow," I say, stepping back to let them by. The back door opens and everyone spills out of the kitchen. My mom puts the flowers she's carrying on the counter and looks around. Claire is grinning like crazy.

"It looks great," my mom says, smiling around at the shop and then at Jan. My mom and Jan have only seen each other half a dozen times and always for about ten seconds when she's picking me up or he's dropping me off. "It's so warm and friendly in here and well—" She pauses. "Amazing."

"Thank you," Jan says. He's quiet for a moment. "The flowers are beautiful."

"Oh," my mother says. "The flowers are for you. For your show."

I walk over to where Jillian and Claire are standing, leaving Jan and my mother talking about why roses don't have scents anymore. I've already heard that discussion about a thousand times. Claire is smiling at my mom and Jan.

"What?" I ask, elbowing her.

"Nothing," she says, but she keeps grinning, reminding me a little too much of Jillian when she's devising some scheme.

Jillian clears her throat. "You guys should come to my house to get ready for the Umlaut event."

"She means so she can supervise us as we're getting ready," Claire says to me.

"What are you going to wear?" Jillian asks me.

"I don't know," I say. The truth is I haven't had time to think of much other than candy and homework and swimming. "I'll figure it out."

Jillian stares at me for almost a full minute. I shift under her gaze, wondering what I've said this time that has her looking at me like I'm from some other planet. One apparently without fancy art openings and posh fund-raisers. "I'll take care of it," she says. "All you have to do is be at my house by six."

I look around to be sure no one else is listening. "Have you told Charlie?" I ask.

She shakes her head. "I want it to be a surprise," she says. I know for a fact that Charlie hates surprises, but before I can say anything I hear my mother's phone ringing. She takes it out and looks at it. She smiles apologetically at Jan before turning to answer it. "Is everything okay?" she asks into the phone.

I start to tell Jillian again that she should give Charlie the heads up about the Umlaut thing, but the look on my mother's face makes me pause. "How high?" my mother asks. She looks over at me. "I'll be right there." She hangs up. To Jan she says, "I'm sorry. That was my sitter. It seems my other two children are sick. Both with fevers."

"Oh no," Jan says. "Poor little guys."

"I'll get my coat," I say. I head into the back and grab my jacket from the hook. My mother is still talking to Jan when I come back.

"No, no. I'm a ginger ale girl when I'm sick," my mother says. I walk over. "So is Piper."

"And I would have picked you as a Sprite person," Jan says, smiling at me. He picks up a bag from the counter and drops two of his new ring pops into it. He hands it to my mother. "For when they feel better."

"I'm sure they'll love them," she says. "Thank you."

"Break a leg tomorrow," I tell Jan as he holds the door open for us.

He smiles at me. "Hopefully not literally." He stands watching us as we climb into the car. He waves as we pull away and closes the door behind him. I can see inside the shop where everyone is back to work moving and arranging and straightening.

"He's a nice man," my mother says, pulling out onto the street.

"He is nice," I say. I glance over at my mother. She reaches across and squeezes my hand. I squeeze back. We ride in silence all the way home, but it's a good quiet. Peaceful.

I push open the front door and notice two things immediately. First, the bunch of balloons that were delivered to my house is now down to just one balloon. There were a dozen, six orange and six yellow. My two favorite colors. The other thing I notice is that the house is quiet, eerily quiet.

Mrs. Bateman meets us in the hall, actually looking better than usual. "They're both sleeping," she says. "I just checked on them." She keeps talking to my mother about their temperatures and who ate what and who threw up when. I walk through the living room and open one of the windows. The air from outside wafts through, making the house smell a bit better and making my last balloon bob in the breeze.

"Piper," Mrs. Bateman says from the door. "I'm sorry about your balloons," she says. "They were . . . well, I was able to save one of them." I smile in thanks. One is more than I would have guessed. My mother closes the door behind her and then heads upstairs. I follow her up and peek into Dom and Lucy's room. They are both sacked out in their beds. They always look so little when they're asleep. More so when they are sick and asleep. Dom rolls over and reaches a hand out to me. I take it. It's hot against my skin.

"Hi," I say softly.

"Hi," he whispers. "I feel yucky."

"I know," I say, sitting on the edge of his bed. I take the cold pack that Mrs. Bateman gave him and hold it on his forehead.

"Sorry about the balloons," Dom says.

"Did you pop them?" I ask, knowing they like to run around and torment each other with the threat of the sudden, loud noise of a popping balloon.

Dom shakes his head and the cold pack slips over one eye. I push it back up onto his forehead. "We let them go," he says.

"Did they go high?"

He smiles at me and nods. "Where do you think they'll land?"

I pretend to think. "France," I say.

"Really?"

I shrug. "Maybe," I say. Dom closes his eyes. When his breathing deepens, I start to stand up, but his hand grabs at mine again.

"Piper, don't hate Valentine's Day," he says. I sigh and look down at him. His eyes are still closed. "I'll be your Valentine."

"I'd like that," I say, tears springing to my eyes. I wait another moment then walk to the hallway, where my mother is standing. She takes my hand and squeezes it. "They can be very sweet," I say.

She laughs softly. "Yeah, when they're running fevers."

"Well it's better than nothing," I say, smiling. Mom pulls the door slightly closed to keep the light from the hall out of their room. I yawn, covering my mouth with my hand.

Mom pushes me toward my room. "Now you," she says. "Bed."

"Yes, ma'am." She swats me lightly on the shoulder as I pass. I lie on my bed completely clothed, too exhausted to change into my pajamas. I feel like I could sleep for a hundred years. Unfortunately I only get to sleep for an hour before the sound of throwing up and crying wakes me. I stumble out to the hall, my eyes still half-closed.

My mother is holding Dom's head over the toilet.

"Mommy!" Lucy calls from the bedroom. I walk in. "Piper, I feel—" But she doesn't finish. She just bursts into tears. I pick her up out of bed and walk with her to my mother's bathroom. I stay with her while she gets sick. By the time we get everything cleaned up and Dom and Lucy back in bed, I'm wide awake. I take a shower and pull on my pajamas. As I pass my desk, a slip of paper flutters to the ground. I pick it up. It's my father's number. I tuck it under the edge of the paperweight and climb back into bed. I will myself to sleep, but it seems the more you need to sleep, the less you can. I push back the covers and grab my sweatshirt. I slide open my window and climb out onto the roof, careful not to make too much noise. Even so, I hear Charlie's window slide open and then him stepping across the space between our houses.

"Stay upwind from me," I say. "I may be infected."

"How are they?" he asks.

"Yucky," I say, stealing their word.

Charlie nods. "How are you?"

I take a deep breath. "I'm good," I say. Charlie is quiet. He knows me well enough to know that good is never good. "You seem to be getting along with Jillian," I say.

Charlie doesn't say anything for a few moments. "Jillian is nice," he says finally. I try to read his tone of voice, but I can't. I look out over our neighborhood. Blue lights flicker in some of the windows. People watching television. A car alarm goes off a few streets away; then it's gone as quickly as it began.

"Do you ever wish you could know what other people's lives are like?" I ask.

"I don't know if you can ever know," Charlie says.

"But if you could," I say.

Charlie is quiet for a long moment. "No," he says finally.

"Why not?" I ask.

"Because that would go both ways," he says. "Other

people would be able to see inside your life too." I think about all the things I wouldn't want anyone to know about me.

"Yeah," I say. "I guess you're right." We sit for a long while, just watching the blinking lights in front of us. Looking up I spot a star twinkling in the otherwise dark sky. "First star," I say. Charlie doesn't respond. "What did you wish for?" I prompt. He's quiet for so long, I don't think he's going to answer.

"I'm not sure I believe in wishes," he says.

"What?" I ask with mock horror in my voice. "You're the king of wishes. I mean, your last name is Wish. Man." I figure that will get a smile out of him, but he's quiet again.

"I'm going to—" Then without saying anything else, Charlie gets up and walks back across the roof and climbs in through his window. I sit still, my chin on my knees. I feel an ache in my chest, but even if someone offered me a million dollars, I'm not sure I could say exactly why.

chapter fifteen

The halls are filled to the brim with students hurrying to do nothing during break. I quickly spin the lock on my locker.

"What is it?" Jillian asks from behind me.

"Be patient," I say, pulling my locker open. The bag propped on my books is bigger than the other ones have been. Jillian reaches around me, impatiently, and pulls out the bag. She looks inside.

"What is it?" Claire asks, hurrying toward us. Jillian tilts the bag so she can see inside. "Flip-flops?" She looks at me. I shrug and pull out the books I need for my morning classes.

"You love flip-flops," Claire says, as if I need reminding. I am the Queen of Flip-Flops. I own easily twenty pairs. Most of them are like the ones in Jillian's hand. Cheap and brightly colored.

♥ **love?** maybe.

"I guess they're cool," Jillian says, but her voice has lost its enthusiasm.

"Caff or front lawn?" Claire asks. The day is really sunny and warm, but I need something to drink and vote for the caff.

While Claire and Jillian grab a table, I get in line for the coffee bar. I order mochas for Claire and Jillian and a cup of orange tea for me. For some reason coffee just doesn't sound very good. As I carry the drinks to where Jillian and Claire are sitting, I see Stuart over in the corner with a bunch of soccer players. Thankfully Christi isn't with him. I sit down across from Claire. She looks at me and shakes her head a little.

"Look," Claire says, pointing over to a table where dozens of people are waiting in line. The crowd parts enough to allow us to read the sign hung across the front of the table.

I roll my eyes. "I'd forgotten about the Student Council carnations," I say. Jillian tilts her head at me. I remember this is her first Valentine's Day at Montrose. "Every year, the student council sells carnations for a dollar each. Then during homeroom, they go around and tie them to everyone's locker."

"And that's bad because . . ."

"You'll see," Claire says. I nod, remembering last year. For the three days leading up to Valentine's Day all anyone could talk about was how many flowers they got. Claire got thirteen. One from me. Twelve from Stuart. I got two. One from Claire and a pity flower from Stuart.

"It's awful," I say. "Just another scam to make single people feel even more alone and isolated."

"I'll buy you a flower," Claire says. I smile at her.

"Thanks," I say. I hate to admit it but, even if *I* had to buy my own flower, I probably would. A totally empty locker is social suicide.

"What are you worried about?" Jillian asks me. "You have Ben Donovan. I have no one."

Claire sits quietly for a moment, staring at her lap. "Jillian, you have Jeremy and Charlie and probably half of the freshman class," she says. She looks up at us. "*I* have no one."

"You're wrong," I say. "You have us." Claire gives me a smile.

"Piper's right," Jillian says. "You have us. And don't pay attention to me. I have no idea what I'm talking about half the time anyway."

"True," Claire says, elbowing her. Jillian pretends to be hurt, but she can't keep from smiling.

"I can't wait until tomorrow night," Jillian says.

"Tell me you told Charlie," I say. I thought about telling him last night, but then it got so weird.

"I told you," Jillian says. "It's a surprise."

I take a deep breath and start to tell her *again* that Charlie doesn't like surprises, but Claire beats me to it. "Charlie hates surprises."

"Everyone—" Jillian begins, but Claire and I are both shaking our heads.

"We tried to throw him a surprise birthday party in seventh grade," I say.

"He wouldn't talk to us for a month."

Jillian sighs. "I'll call him," she says.

I check my watch. "You'll have to leave a message," I say. "He's still at swim practice."

"Every time I try to call him, he's in the pool," Jillian says, making me wonder how often she tries to call him.

I guess Claire wonders the same thing. "So, are you two spending a lot of time together?"

Jillian just smiles as she pulls out her phone. She starts texting. "I'm just telling him I have a surprise for him," she says. She puts the phone on the table and takes a sip of her mocha. A rooster crows as her phone lights up. She holds it up and looks at it. It makes me feel funny that she has one of Charlie's weird ring tones. That's always been something he's done for me. "He says he can't wait." I look over at Claire, who just shrugs. "Guess you two don't know him as well as you think you do," she says.

"I guess not," Claire says.

"Guess not," I say. I take a sip of my tea, savoring the warmth on my throat. I feel a lot like I did a year ago when Charlie's dad was talking about the two of them relocating to California. It feels like he might be moving, but now it's not across the country. It's just away from me.

♡ ♡ ♡

Jan texts me during fifth period. I've been dying to call him all day to find out how everything with the Food Network went, but I haven't had two seconds to myself. Luckily I have the sounds on my phone turned off, because Mrs. Beckensail doesn't just confiscate your phone for the rest of the period if she catches you using it, she keeps it overnight.

Need help.
—Jan

That can't be good, I think, tucking my phone back into the front pocket of my backpack. I try to call him back after class, but both his cell and the store phone click immediately over to voice mail. I finally just text him.

B there @ 4.
—P

I find Jillian after fifth period and ask her to come to Jan's with me. If things went badly with the Food Network people, I might need help cheering him up. I spend all of sixth period trying to imagine what could have happened. Short of accidentally pouring boiling sugar on the host or finding a cockroach mixed in with the caramels, I can't come up with a single reason why Jan needs my help. Turns out Jeremy can't either. When I find Jillian after school, Jeremy's with her. He got the same text I did.

We start walking toward the bus stop. Jillian calls her

mother and tells her not to pick her up at school.

"Sounded like picking me up was the last thing on her mind anyway. I probably didn't even need to call."

"Yes, you are utterly forgettable," Jeremy says. Jillian shakes her head at him, but she's smiling when she does it. I call my mother to tell her I'll be home right after I stop by Jan's. I agreed to take over for Mrs. Bateman after school.

"Take your time," my mother says.

"But I thought Mrs. Bateman had to leave at five."

"She does, but I found someone else to cover for her."

"Who?" I ask, wondering who my mother could possibly convince to sit with the vomit twins.

"Beau." If my mother had said she got Mary Poppins to watch them, I wouldn't have been more surprised. She starts laughing when I don't say anything. "I know," she says. "He called this morning to talk about the weekend and I told him the kids were sick. He volunteered to come right over."

"And you're sure he did?" I ask.

"Yes, Piper," my mother says. "I just got off the phone with him. He was reading to them when I called."

"Wow," is all I can think to say.

"Sometimes people surprise you," she says. "Oh, I talked to Jan earlier. He sounded *stressed*." Since when is Mom talking to Jan? "So, listen. Call me when you're finished. I'll come get you."

The bus pulls up, sending a cloud of exhaust over us. Jillian and Jeremy race to the back like they're little kids. "What, no animals this time?" the driver asks me. It's the same one that let me bring Chi Chi on board.

"Not this time," I say. I drop into the seat behind the driver. Jillian and Jeremy don't seem to notice I'm not sitting with them. Jeremy is telling Jillian something that is making her laugh so hard she's having a hard time breathing. I lean back in the seat and think about what my mom said, about how people can surprise you. I look back at Jeremy and Jillian still laughing. I mean, that's a surprise. And Beau actually volunteering to take care of the kids is a surprise. And Ben Donovan asking me out is a surprise. But so is my dad calling after two years and Stuart cheating on Claire. It's too bad people surprise you in bad ways as much as in good ways.

The bus hits a bump hard. Jillian screams, then laughs. I hear Jeremy telling her to stop embarrassing him and her laughing again. I yank the cord above my head when we get close to Commerce Avenue. The bus slows down. Jillian and Jeremy are up and past me before I can even pick up my backpack. I follow them down the sidewalk, watching my feet passing across the cracks where grass has pushed up through the concrete. I almost run into the back of Jeremy, who is stopped right in the middle of the walkway.

"What are you—" I look up at the parking lot in front of Jan's. It's jammed with several vans and a big truck with what looks like a satellite dish on the top of it. "They're still here?" I ask. We push through the crowd gathered on the sidewalk in front of the shop. A man with sunglasses on puts his hand out, stopping us.

"They're filming," he says. We can see Jan talking to a man wearing a bowling shirt. He's pouring sugar syrup into the big copper kettle he has hanging in the window. A tray of apples with sticks poking out of the top of them is on the table beside the kettle. Bowling Shirt Guy picks up an apple and dips it into the kettle as Jan talks. He gives the apple a twist and deposits it back on the tray, but now it's covered in a thin layer of red candy. Jan looks up. He sees us and says something to the man still dipping apples, who turns to the cameraman. He makes a slicing gesture across his throat and the cameraman lowers the camera. Bowling Shirt Guy motions us inside. Sunglasses Man steps aside and holds the door for us.

The guy with the bowling shirt reaches us first, his hand out. "You must be Jeremy," he says. Jeremy shakes hands with him. "Piper?" He turns to Jillian, but she just shakes her head and backs up. He looks over at me.

"Yes," I say, taking his hand. He shakes it, but doesn't let go of it. Instead he pulls me to the counter.

"Talk to me," he says. He motions to the cameraman, who lifts the camera. "Oh, is it okay if we film you?" he asks. I nod, not sure what else to do.

"This is just the initial run-through. We'll get you into hair and makeup when we actually start filming the segment." I look over at Jan, but he's just smiling at me. Bowling Shirt

Guy gestures at the cameraman again and a red light on the camera comes on. "So Piper Paisley, tell me how you came up with your idea for breakfast-flavored taffy." My brain freezes and all I can do is repeat his question in my head then the word breakfast over and over. I look to Jan for help, but he tilts his head at me and grins.

"Well," I say, taking a deep breath. "I got the idea from my little sister." I talk about some of the other candy I've developed. The condiment taffy collection. He tries one of the relish-flavored ones and smiles.

"It's surprisingly good. Tell me about these," he says, holding up a box of my Consternation Hearts. He pours some into his hand and the cameraman comes over and films the candy close-up. A silver heart is nestled in his hand along with the pastel Consternation Hearts. I glance over at Jan, but he won't meet my gaze.

Jeremy is next. He talks about his bacon truffles and other things I didn't even know he was working on: chocolate-covered potato chips, chocolate-covered pickles. He talks about why he decided that dark chocolate was a better match for the pickles, but that the chips needed milk chocolate. Jillian sits at one of the tables. I worry for a moment that she feels left out, but the Food Network guy asks if she can help with some of the demo work, dipping apples, pulling taffy, tempering chocolate. While we get our hair and makeup done, which only Jillian seems to enjoy, someone calls all of our parents, making sure they have permission to put us on television. We each have to sign a lot of forms, which our parents will also have to sign before they can air the show.

"We're in sort of a rush," one of the producers tells us. "We were just going to do a short segment for our *Tastes of America* show, but when we got here, we realized that this place is a gold mine. We're actually going put together a Valentine's Day special and then tomorrow, we're going to film an episode of *Sweets* here. The host is flying in late tonight from the Aspen Food and Wine Festival." I keep nodding as all the information washes over me.

"Jan," I say when we're all made up and standing around waiting, "I think you might need to go ahead and get that expansion thing going."

"I'm way ahead of you, Piper," he says. I don't have time to ask him what he means before the host is pulling him over to the front counter and the camera starts rolling. One thing I find out right off the bat is that it takes way longer than thirty minutes to film a half-hour-long show. The producer calls a break after they finally finish with Jan.

"We need food," one of the lighting guys says. "Anyone know where we can get good pizza around here?"

"I do," I say. We call Artie's and order twenty large pizzas.

"That's a lot even for you," Artie says.

"Ha-ha," I say. I tell him what's going on. He tells me he'll deliver them personally. "I'm sure," I say, smirking.

My mother brings Claire by once they are finished at the

flower shop. She comes in, intending to stay just a moment, but one of the producers corners her when she finds out the flowers are hers. She talks with her for a while. I notice Jan smiling at my mother the whole time. She finally tells the producer she has to go, that she has sick kids to get home to.

She comes over to me and puts her arm around me. "Another surprise," she says.

"Another good one," I say. She looks at me for a moment like she wants to ask something, but then she shakes her head.

"Call me when you're done," she says. "I'll come get you."

"I'll bring her home," Jan says. "I don't want you to have to bring those kids out when they're sick."

"Thank you," she says. They stand smiling at each other for a moment.

"I'll walk you out," Jan says to my mother.

The pizzas arrive, delivered by Artie as promised. I notice he makes a point of talking to the host of the show. He gives him a business card before he leaves. He mouths *thank you* to me on the way out the door.

Everyone falls on the pizzas, which I notice are all heart-shaped. I grab a box and Jeremy, Jillian, Claire, and I retreat to the kitchen. If anyone but me feels the absence of Charlie, they don't say anything.

"You guys are going to be on television," Claire says. "You'll be celebrities."

"Don't worry, Claire," Jeremy says. "We won't forget the

little people." Claire rolls her eyes at him. We eat in silence, all too hungry and too tired to do much else. Jan comes in after a while and I wonder if he was talking to my mother the whole time. He grabs a slice of pizza, but I notice he only takes a couple of bites before he puts it back down. He puts his hands in his pockets and rocks on his feet as he jingles the keys in his pocket.

"You'd better not do that while they're filming," Jillian says.

"Good point," he says. "Now I know why I pay you—"

"You don't pay me anything," Jillian says.

"You get free pizza," Jeremy points out.

"True. But I would do this without the free pizza," Jillian says. We all nod.

"I know you would," Jan says. "I am—"

"Very grateful," we all say.

Jan laughs. "Well, I am." He walks over to his desk and empties his pockets, dumping his wallet, his keys, a handkerchief, and about seven dollars in change on the mound of things already threatening to overflow onto the floor.

The door to the front opens and one of the producers sticks her head in. "We're ready," she says, and lets the door close again.

Jan claps his hands together. "See you out there," he says, and pushes through the door into the shop. Jeremy folds up the now-empty pizza box and pushes it into the recycling bin next to Jan's desk. The little bump he gives the desk is all it takes to start the avalanche. A rain of coins and papers falls to the floor.

"Dang it," Jeremy says, making Jillian laugh.

"What, are you a cowboy now?" Jillian asks, smirking at him. She gestures at the coins and papers all around us. "Leave it. You have a segment to film." Jeremy thanks her and pushes out into the shop. Claire, Jillian, and I spend the next few minutes crawling around on the floor, picking up coins and restacking papers.

"I think that's it," Claire says, standing up and dusting off her hands.

"Do I have any pizza in my teeth?" I ask, baring them at her. She takes a look and shakes her head. She does the same for Jillian and then bares her teeth at us.

"Good thing they aren't filming us now," I say. "That would be weird." We start toward the door to the front. I stop and look at Jillian. "So, what's going on with you and Jeremy?" I ask.

"What do you mean?" she replies, her voice letting on she knows *exactly* what I mean.

"You two just seem very—"

"Chummy," Claire finishes.

"Chummy?" I ask. Claire smiles and shrugs. "Okay," I say, turning back to look at Jillian. "What's with the chummy?" She starts to answer, but the door opens and the same producer who called Jan pokes her head through.

"I'm sorry, girls, but we need to get going if we're

going to wrap by midnight." We all head toward the door.

The host says my segment went well, even though they had to make me redo it three times. "Don't worry. My first show was a disaster," he says. "It took them four days to get twenty minutes of useable footage." I'm not sure if he's telling the truth, but it does make me feel better. "Your Consternation Hearts are brilliant," he says, making me smile. "That spot of hope in the middle of all that cynicism. Pure genius." He walks away, leaving me wondering what he's talking about.

I'm half asleep by the time they finish filming. Jan talks to the producer for a few minutes about the next day. We promise to stop by after school in case they need anything more from us.

We all pile into Jan's hearse. He drops off Jeremy, then Claire, then Jillian. I'm last. I notice Beau's truck isn't there when we pull up.

"Thanks again, Piper," Jan says.

"You're welcome," I say. I cover my mouth as a big yawn escapes.

"Get some sleep," Jan says. "Five A.M. isn't that far away." I groan. I'd forgotten about swim practice. "Plus, I don't want you to go to that fancy shindig with dark circles under your eyes." I nod and climb out of the car. Knowing Jan's watching, I don't slow down when I look over at Charlie's. All the windows are dark. Of course they would be; it's almost one in the morning. Jan waits until I'm inside and the door is firmly shut behind me. I bump through the kitchen and the living room in the dark, trying to make as little noise as possible. That works until I get to my room. There's something big floating right in my doorway. My scream sends my mother flying out of her room. She snaps on the hall lights.

"What in the world?" she asks.

I start laughing as soon as my eyes adjust to the bright light. Bobbing, tied to my desk chair is the one balloon. "Sorry," I say. "The balloon—"

"No wonder I'm starting to go gray," she says, shaking her head. "Still no idea who the balloons were from?" she asks.

I shake my head. "There wasn't a note."

"Since there doesn't seem to be an emergency, I'm going back to bed." Before she pulls her door shut, she turns and gives me her best mom look. "I suggest you go to bed as well."

"Yes, ma'am," I say, smiling. She shakes her head and shuts the door between us, making the balloon bob around like crazy. I'm half tempted to open the window and release it.

As I climb into bed, I remember that I was supposed to call Ben Donovan. *I am now the girl who forgets to call Ben Donovan,* I think. But as I fall asleep, it's Jillian that I can't get out of my head. All night I couldn't help but notice that Jillian was quieter than usual after we ate. And she kept looking at Jeremy, a half smile on her face, like she wanted to say something to him but wasn't sure how.

chapter sixteen

Jan was right. Five A.M. comes way too early. Charlie is waiting in his car in front of my house as I stumble outside. I toss my bag in the backseat and climb in front.

Charlie starts the car and pulls away from the curb. He looks over at me. "You look like—" Charlie says.

"Tired," I say. "The word you're looking for is tired."

"Um-hum," Charlie says, turning off our street and onto Commerce. "Listen, I'm sorry I've been kind of acting weird for a while now—"

"Yeah, like the last seven years," I say.

Charlie laughs. "She's still got a smart mouth even when she's half dead. No really, I—"

"Charlie, we're good," I say.

"You sure?" he asks.

"Mm hmm," I say, leaning my face against the window. It

feels cool against my cheek. I must fall asleep, because the next thing I know Charlie is pulling up in front of the Montrose Natatorium.

"Hey, sleeping beauty. We're here." I groan and look out the windshield at the building hulking over us.

"Stupid place," I say, pushing the door open. I pull my bag out of the backseat and sling it over my shoulder. "Stupid swimming," I say. A group of guys jostle me as they walk past. "Stupid swimmers."

"You really are grouchy when you haven't gotten enough sleep," Charlie says.

"Zip it," I say. This just makes Charlie laugh. "I hate you right now," I say.

"No you don't, Piper. You love me." He's quiet, making me look over at him. His whole face is quickly turning red. "Anyway," he says, turning back to look through the windshield. "Have a good swim." I push the door shut and heft my bag onto my shoulder

"Weird," I say under my breath. I watch as Charlie pulls away and heads across town to his own school and his own pool and his own swim practice. Once I'm swimming, I forget all about Charlie and being tired. All I can focus on is making it from one end of the pool to the other. After the workout, Coach yells at us all for about ten minutes, telling us we're a bunch of weak, unmotivated, lazy teenagers, which in general we are. We just nod, waiting for him to finish. Finally he stops yelling and just stares at us for several moments.

"Hit the showers," he says. Then he storms off the deck. I wave feebly at Peter and Ben Donovan. I spend the rest of practice curled up on one of the tables in the training room.

It isn't until the bell ending zero period rings that I wake up. I sit up and push my hair out of my face. I reach into my backpack and get one of the two bananas I grabbed from our kitchen counter before I left. Maybe if I eat something, I'll feel better.

I stumble down the hall toward homeroom, nibbling on the banana.

"Piper?" I turn and see Ben Donovan walking toward me. I am painfully aware that I've definitely looked better. "You okay?" he asks. I nod, my mouth full of a bite of banana. I reach into my backpack and pull out the other banana. I hold it toward him, swallowing.

"Want one?" I ask, thinking about the banana someone left in my locker.

"Sure," he says, taking it from me. I watch him to see if there is any reaction, but there's nothing. The bell for homeroom rings, saving me from saying anything weird. "I'll see you tonight," he says. He leans toward me and for a brief moment, I imagine he's going to kiss me right there in the hall, but all he does is brush my hair back from my cheek. He smiles and turns to walk toward his own homeroom. I wait for the jolt, but there's nothing. Maybe I'm just tired. I hurry down the hall, sure I'll be the last person to make it to class, but as I approach the end of the junior wing, I see Claire standing close to someone, talking. She giggles at something he just said. For a wild moment, I think it's Stuart, but then she shifts to one side and I see it's Alex Muñoz. Interesting.

I try to sleep during homeroom, but Claire keeps going on and on about Alex.

"He asked me if I'd come watch him play rugby sometime."

"Yeah, 'cause that wouldn't be weird," I say. "Seeing as how he and Stuart are on the same team."

"I guess," Claire says. I raise my eyebrows at her. She shrugs. "I'm sort of making peace with the whole Stuart thing."

"How Zen of you," I say.

She laughs. "I just figure if Stuart didn't want to be with me anymore, at least I know."

"It's just too bad he didn't have the guts to just tell you instead of sneaking around with Christi behind your back."

Claire shrugs. "In a way, that makes everything even easier. I mean, if he were this great guy, it'd be harder to get over him."

"So you're glad he broke up with you?" I ask

"No," she says. "But I think I will be."

"Like I said. Very Zen."

"Om," she says, closing her eyes and holding her hands out with her thumb and forefinger shaped into little O's.

"Paisley. Jenkins. If you want to do yoga, please do so on your own time," Mr. Reyes says from the front of the room. The whole class looks over at us and laughs. Claire and I start laughing too, earning a dirty look from Mr. Reyes. Luckily the bell rings just then and we scoot out the door as fast as we can. We start toward my locker. Since I was sound asleep until about four minutes before homeroom, I didn't have a chance to go to my locker before.

"Hey, princess!"

Claire nudges me. "I think he means you." I look over and see Barry (I mean Booger) standing with a group of Pitters.

"You must be an awesome kisser," he says. Every bone in my body tells me to keep walking, but my brain disagrees. I stop and look at him.

"What are you talking about, *Barry*?"

"Just saying you must be *good* to get that many flowers." All the Pitters laugh. I look over at Claire, who shrugs. I shake my head at him and turn away. We walk down the hall, but as soon as we round the corner, a crowd of people forces us to stop.

"What's going on?" I ask. Claire shrugs again. We try to push through the group of people huddled near my locker. Jillian spots us and pushes toward us.

"Okay, now, *this* is the most romantic thing I've ever heard of."

"What are you—" She pulls me through the rest of the crowd and up to my locker. At least I think it's my locker. It's so covered in flowers that they've even spilled over onto the lockers on either side of mine. Someone from student council is still threading flowers into the vents in my locker.

"You'll have to tell your boyfriend I did the best I could," he says, handing me a bunch of orange carnations. "It's supposed to be a heart."

"I can tell," I say, looking at the clusters of flowers poking out here and there. Although to be honest I wouldn't have been sure if he hadn't told me.

"How many?" Jillian asks.

"Thirty," he says.

"Wow," I say.

"Who are they from?" Jillian asks, smirking at me. I know she's still *sure* it's Ben Donovan, but after our latest encounter, I feel just as sure it's not him.

The student council guy looks surprised. "Her boyfriend," he says.

"But I don't have a boyfriend," I say.

"Well some guy then."

"Describe him," Jillian demands.

"Can't," he says. "All we got was an envelope with thirty bucks in it and a locker number and instructions to put the flowers in a heart shape. Mrs. Craig in the front office gave it to us. Said someone dropped it off yesterday afternoon."

"We want the note," Jillian says. The student council guy steps back a little, clearly afraid of her intensity. She looks at me and Claire. "For handwriting analysis."

"Don't mind my friend," I say to the rapidly retreating student council guy. "She thinks she's on CSI Montrose."

He nods, smiling. "Tell your boyfriend thanks," he says. He pauses and smiles at me. "When you find out who he is."

I manage to push between the flowers and get into my locker. We decide to head to the caff for break. I put my head down as soon as we sit at a table. Jillian can't stop guessing who might have given me the flowers. "It *has* to be Ben Donovan," she says. I shake my head and tell her about the banana encounter. She claims that it doesn't rule him out, but I can hear the doubt in her voice. She frowns for a moment, but then her face brightens. "More intrigue," she says.

"The carnations were orange. Orange is one of your favorite colors," Claire says.

"Claire, are you leaving the gifts?" I ask, thinking that she seems to already know why the gifts are my favorite.

"I'm not," she says. "I promise." I look over at her and smile. She's telling the truth. Claire is as bad a liar as I am.

"Let's examine the evidence," Jillian says. I roll my eyes, but she ignores me. "He's a true romantic. He has access to your locker." She ticks them off on her fingers. "He seems to really know you." She trails off with only three fingers in the air.

"Peter Finch?" Claire asks. We all look over to the other side of the room where Peter is flexing his arm for Sarah.

"Eww," I say. "No."

"Then who?" Jillian asks again. I shrug. Part of me still thought it was Jillian or Claire, but they are both genuinely baffled.

Claire interrupts Jillian's investigation to tell her all about her phone call with Alex Muñoz. Since I've already heard everything, I don't feel bad about putting my head down on my arms.

"It's all coming together," Jillian says.

"What's coming together?" I ask, looking up at her.

"The Plan!" Jillian says.

"What plan?" I ask, just to annoy her.

"*The* Plan!" she says again, clearly annoyed.

"Oh," Claire says. "You mean the love potion plan?"

"And the flirting plan?"

"And the makeover plan?" Claire asks. Jillian frowns.

Claire reaches out and touches her hand. "It was a good plan," she says. She smiles. "Even though nothing worked."

"But we do all have very good prospects for Valentine's Day," Jillian points out.

"Good thing, because it's only a few days away," I say.

Jillian nods. "I mean, I have Charlie and sort of Jeremy." She looks at Claire. "And you have Alex Muñoz—"

"I don't think one phone call—"

"Humor her," I say.

"Okay, *you sort* of have Alex." She pokes my elbow. "And Piper is the big winner. Ben Donovan."

"Mm hmm," I say, thinking about falling asleep again.

"Okay," Jillian says. "After school we go by Jan's and then we go to my place to get ready." She pokes me again. "I have *the best* dress for you. Ben Donovan is going to freak."

"Ben Donovan is going to freak about what?" a male voice asks. I look up and see Ben Donovan coming up behind Jillian. Jillian turns ten shades of pink which is sort of funny. I was under the impression that Jillian didn't have the capacity for embarrassment. Ben Donovan smiles at me. "How are you feeling?" he asks.

"Okay," I say. "I'm just really, really tired." I scoot over so he can sit down.

"I just came to see what time you wanted me to pick you up tonight, but maybe you aren't feeling—"

"She'll be fine by then," Jillian says.

I smile over at him and nod. "I'll be fine by then." Ben Donovan puts his hand on mine. I look at him holding my hand. Maybe it's just because I'm super tired, but I still don't feel a thing.

"So what time?" he asks.

"Meet us there seven-ish," Jillian says. "I'll have them hold your badge at the front in case you get there before us."

"Cool," Ben Donovan says. "I'm looking forward to it." He squeezes my hand. "Guess I better—" He nods toward where a bunch of swimmers are clustered around Peter, who is now trying to cram as many Oreos in his mouth at the same time as he can. It makes me think of Charlie. Ben Donovan gets up and gives me one more smile. *It's a nice smile,* I think before putting my head back on my arms.

"He is *so* yummy," Jillian says. She pokes my elbow, making me look up. "You guys make such a cute couple." I nod, but then I notice Claire sitting there looking at me, her left eyebrow raised just a tiny bit higher than the other. I smile at her. *Claire's back,* I think. I can't ever get anything by her. I can maybe fake Jillian out and make her believe that I'm head over heels for Ben Donovan, but not Claire. I smile into my arms. *I am now the girl who just isn't that into Ben Donovan.* Life just keeps throwing me surprises.

Too bad they aren't always good surprises. Mom texts me, asking me to call her at the shop when I get a chance. I slip outside during lunch and sit on a cement bench under one of the trees.

"Hi," I say. "What's up?"

"Where are you?" she asks. She might as well ask *Are you sitting down?*

"Outside the library," I say. "Sitting on a bench." Mom takes a deep breath. "Just tell me or ask me," I say. "Wait, are Dom and Lucy okay?"

"Yes, they're fine. Beau's with them. I'm sorry, Piper. It's just weird. It's Jack," she says. I don't say anything. "Your father."

"Yes, Mom. I know my father's name."

She makes a sort of nervous giggle noise. "It's just that he called again this morning. He said he really wants to talk to you. He asked for your cell number, but I just didn't feel right giving him that."

"What does he want, Mom? I mean, after all this time?"

"I don't know, Pipe. He said he has something to talk to you about."

"I'll call him, Mom," I say. "Just not today. I've got so much going on and I'm wiped. I feel like I need to be on top of my game when I talk to Jack."

Mom laughs for real this time. "Yes, that's probably a good plan. Talking to Jack is always like playing dodgeball with an octopus. You need to have really good reflexes to react to whatever he's going to throw at you."

This makes me laugh. "Pretty clever, Mom," I say.

"I can bring it when I need to," she says.

"All right, you can put the teen slang dictionary back on the shelf," I say. "You're starting to creep me out." The bell signaling the end of lunch rings. "I need to go," I say. "I'll call you from Jan's."

"Jack's not all bad, Piper."

I sigh. "I know." And I do. Jack was always the fun parent. He taught me how to skateboard and spit cherry pits and make mud pies.

"I love you," Mom says, interrupting my memories.

"I love you too," I say, and end the call. I hope the next surprise is a good one. Or maybe just no more surprises for a bit. That would be fine too.

Jan's is still mobbed with people when we get there. Mostly TV people, but a lot of regular people too. Jan's made the local news this morning. The *Good Morning Atlanta* van is still parked in front. This time the guy at the door just smiles at us and steps aside to let us in, earning a lot of complaints from the crowd, who are all forced to observe from the sidewalk. Jillian grabs my arm hard when we enter.

"Ow," I say, trying to pry her fingers from my forearm, but she keeps a tight grip as she stares at where Jan is talking to some guy in a flannel shirt and jeans. He turns and we can see the side of his face. I start laughing.

"What's so funny?" Jeremy asks.

"Tell him," I say, elbowing Jillian. She just shakes her head. Her cheeks are bright pink.

"Last fall . . ." I begin. "Okay, it's sort of stupid, but it was late and we were bored." Jeremy makes an impatient movement with his hand. "Anyway, Claire and I were hanging at Jillian's watching television." Jeremy makes the hand motion again. "So Jillian makes us pick a TV boyfriend." Jeremy squints at me. "You know, someone on television who we'd want to be our boyfriend if you know . . ."

"You magically fell through the screen and into TV land," Jeremy says.

"Uh-huh," I say. "So anyway, Jillian picked him." I gesture toward the guy talking to Jan.

Jeremy looks over at Nerdy Flannel Guy. "Him?" he asks. Jillian nods, her cheeks still pink. "But he's . . ." He struggles to find the right word.

"A nerd," I finish. Jeremy nods, clearly surprised.

"So you *like* nerdy guys?" he asks Jillian. She shrugs.

Jan sees us standing there and beckons us over. He quickly introduces us to Jillian's TV boyfriend. Jeremy and I say hello. Jillian tries, but can't manage more than a smile. Jan looks at her for a long moment, clearly wondering what we did with the real Jillian.

"Heard you guys were the big stars yesterday," Nerdy Flannel Guy says. None of us knows what to say to that. "So, which one of you came up with this?" he asks, pointing to the bacon truffles.

"That would be me," Jeremy says.

"Cool," Nerdy Flannel Guy says. "How did you account for the variable fat content of pork products?" Jeremy launches into some complicated formula that creates a ratio of butter fat to protein. He loses me somewhere around the word comestible, but Nerdy Flannel Guy just nods as he listens. Jillian pulls my sleeve and I follow her over to the Valentine's display.

"He's pretty cute, right?" she asks.

"I guess," I say. "He's shorter than I thought he'd be."

Jillian laughs. "I didn't mean *him*. I meant Jeremy." I look over to where Jeremy is still talking and Nerdy Flannel Guy is smiling and nodding.

"Yeah," I say. "He is. But wait. I thought popular jocks were your ideal."

"I thought Ben Donovan was yours," she says in what my mother would say was her *sass voice*. I shake my head. Some part of me is tempted to say touché, but if Ben Donovan isn't my ideal, who is?

chapter seventeen

I don't know about this," I say, pulling at the straps of my dress. Or rather the dress that Jillian picked out for me. "It seems a little . . ."

"Oh no," Jillian says. "You promised when you got here that you would do exactly as I said." I roll my eyes and look back into the full-length mirror hung next to Jillian's closet.

"You look amazing," Claire says from where she is sitting on the bed, holding her phone. She laughs at something on her screen and starts texting back. Alex Muñoz. I look at myself in the mirror. The dress is beautiful—a pale periwinkle color with beading across the hem and up one side, so that it looks like flowers made out of jewels are climbing up one of my legs. I twist to the side. It's my legs that are freaking me out. I'm pretty sure I've only shown more of them on the pool deck in my swimsuit.

♥ love? maybe.

"You sure?" I ask for the seventeenth time.

"Oh my goodness," Jillian says. "Yes!" I smile at myself in the mirror. I do like my hair, and my makeup looks great. As a thank you, the Food Network stylist did all three of our hair and makeup before we left Jan's. "We need to get going," Jillian says, looking at the clock on her bedside table. She points to the pair of heels she put out for me. I swear they look like Cinderella's glass slippers, all crystals and Lucite. I slip them on, wincing a little at the pinch on my toes.

"Girls!" Jillian's mother yells up the stairs. I follow Claire and Jillian out, taking one last look in the mirror as I go. I barely recognize myself. We walk down the stairs toward Jillian's mother, who is standing in the front hall, waiting. This time, I actually do feel like Scarlett O'Hara descending Jillian's stairs. They are long and sweep along one side of their circular entryway. I run my hand down the carved banister to keep from falling and breaking my neck.

Jillian's mother stops us at the bottom and takes a million pictures of us; first individually then the three of us together. I hand her my camera and she takes a dozen with that one too. I promised my mother that I'd get lots of photos. *It's not every day that I get to see you in a dress,* she said when I called her from Jan's.

We all pile into the car parked out front. Jillian's mom can't complain about feeling like our chauffeur this time because there actually is a chauffeur. And while the car isn't a limo, it's the biggest car I've ever been in before and I've been in Jan's hearse plenty of times. We drive the short distance over to the Umlaut event, which is being held outside at the Bernaby Water Gardens.

"Wow," I say as we pull up. The trees surrounding the garden have all been decorated with twinkling strings of white lights and even from inside the car I can hear the harpist that is playing near the entryway. "I really do feel like Cinderella."

"Well," Jillian says, pointing toward the entry. "There's your prince." I lean forward to look out and see Charlie standing near the front, talking to a woman with a clipboard in her hands. He is wearing a tuxedo and his hair is pulled back from his face.

"I, uh . . ." I look over at Claire, who is shaking her head at me. She gestures over to the reception area. *Of course.* Ben Donovan is standing there talking to several girls who all look the same, like they are actually paper dolls who've only recently been separated from one another. "Oh," I say, but I feel something in my stomach. Something that is a little too much like disappointment. *Am I the girl who is now disappointed that she's going on a date with Ben Donovan?*

"Well, this is it," Jillian's mom says as the chauffeur comes around and opens the door. She accepts his hand and steps out of the car. Jillian and Claire follow her. I concentrate on how they do it, so I can attempt to exit the car as gracefully as they do. A big downside to arriving at an event in a fancy car with the president of the foundation is that everyone has turned and is watching us. I manage to climb out with only a slight stumble. Luckily the chauffeur seems used to dealing with klutzy people, and his hand catches me before I wobble too much. I offer him a smile of gratitude. He nods at me and closes the door behind me. I follow Claire and Jillian and Jillian's mother up to the entrance.

"Ready for the stop and repeat?" Jillian points over to the side where people are standing having their photos taken from every angle.

"Seriously?" I ask.

Someone touches my elbow. I look up and see Ben Donovan smiling. "Hi," he says. "You look beautiful." He holds my elbow as we walk over to the group of photographers clustered in front of a banner advertising all of the sponsors for the event.

"Thank you," I say. "This is pretty amazing."

"Um yeah," he says, looking around. Something about the way he says it suggests that he's been to things like this before, maybe a lot before. Jillian has her photo taken by herself, then with her mother, then with her mother and Claire. She manages to pull Charlie in for one shot. Charlie isn't smiling. Then it's my turn. The flashes momentarily blind me as a woman in a black dress guides me and Ben Donovan down the line. She grabs Charlie's arm before he can leave and drags him over beside me. She instructs him to put his arm around me.

"Nice," one of the photographers says, snapping picture after picture. The woman in the dress pulls Ben Donovan away for some individual shots, leaving just Charlie and me.

"Cute couple," an older woman murmurs as we pass. I glance over at Charlie, wondering if he heard her, but he's staring toward the row of cars pulling up to the entrance.

"You look great," I say to Charlie, but it's so loud he doesn't hear me. The blonde woman steers us toward another line where another woman in a black dress hands us our badges and goody bags. One peek inside confirms that these bags are way better than those we used to get at grade school birthday parties. Jillian collects them and gives them to one of the waiters who takes them somewhere for safekeeping.

Ben Donovan is at my side again. "Do you want to go inside?"

I pause, looking around for Charlie, but he's not standing near the entrance anymore. "Sure," I say, surprised at how disappointed I am that Charlie is gone. I let Ben Donovan steer me through the crowd and into the garden. Frank's paintings are hanging on thin wires from the trees. They are lit by soft lights set up in the grass below them. The lighting is so subtle that the paintings almost look like they belong there, as much as the trees and flowers surrounding them. I accept a glass of something gold and bubbly with raspberries in it.

"Ginger ale," Claire says, coming up behind me. Jeremy is with her.

"Hey there," I say. "You clean up good." He does look nice. His suit manages to give him a little more bulk, making him look less scarecrow-ish and more just tall and lean. It turns out Jeremy and Ben Donovan know one another as well.

"We used to swim together," Jeremy says.

"Of course you did," Claire says. Jeremy and Ben Donovan start talking about the Braves and their pennant chances. I shake my head and turn toward Claire.

"Where's Jillian?" I ask. She looks around then shrugs.

"She took off with Charlie as soon as we walked inside. He didn't look happy," she says. "Maybe he doesn't like surprises after all."

"Maybe," I say. We stand around listening to the guys talk sports and watching the beautiful people walk by. We entertain ourselves by trying to decide what work each of the women has had done.

"Botox," Claire says as a woman with a leopard print dress walks by. Her face barely moves when she speaks.

"Clearly," I say. "Eye lift and lip injections," I say about a woman with long blonde hair. Claire nods. "So what else do we do besides stand around?"

"Well, if we had a couple thousand dollars, we could bid on a painting," Claire says. I smile.

"We should go look at them," I say. A sudden gust of wind blows through the garden, making the paintings swing and goose bumps break out on my arms.

Claire looks up at the sky. "I hope it doesn't rain," she says. I look up, seeing long dark clouds whipping across the nearly full moon. I look around at all the artwork hanging in the trees and the beautiful people dripping with diamonds and sipping champagne from tall, thin glasses. Rain would definitely be a bad thing. Claire tells Jeremy and Ben Donovan that we are going to walk around the garden and look at the artwork. They both nod but barely look at us. They're too engrossed in some argument about how designated hitters do or do not ruin the integrity of the game.

"So," Claire says. "Alex texted me a few minutes ago." I smile at her. "He asked if I wanted to go out to dinner on Saturday." She squeezes my arm. "I told him no, of course."

"What?" I ask. "Why? I thought you liked him."

"I'm not going to bail on my best friend on her birthday."

"Oh that," I say. "Claire, it's fine. Let's just do my birthday on Sunday."

"You sure?" she asks. She's trying for nonchalance, like it doesn't matter to her one way or the other, but it's not working that well.

I laugh. "Yes, I am very sure." Claire pulls her phone from her bag and starts typing on it. I turn away to look at one of the paintings, but I'm really looking for Jillian and Charlie. Two women walk up next to me to study the same painting.

"He hasn't arrived yet," one of them says. The other one looks surprised. "Dorian must be getting awfully nervous." Dorian is Jillian's mother. I wonder who hasn't arrived yet.

"Well, you know artist types," the other one says. "I'm sure he's just being dramatic. He'll turn up." They walk down the sidewalk to the next painting.

Claire comes up beside me. She's smiling. "He says he can't wait." I look at her, confused. "Alex," she says.

"Oh. Claire, that's great." I look across the garden again, trying to find Jillian or her mother or Charlie. Or for that matter Charlie's dad.

"What is it?" Claire asks. She smiles at me. "You're looking for Charlie, aren't you?"

I look over at her, seeing a satisfied look on her face. "Well, yeah, but . . ." She continues to smirk at me. "Charlie's dad hasn't shown up yet," I say. Claire is clearly as surprised as I am.

"We should find Charlie," she says. We walk through the garden as quickly as we can considering the crowd and our high heels. We see Jillian's mother talking on her cell phone near the koi pond. She nods at us but turns away, obviously freaked. Another gust of wind, harder this time, whips up the trail. We find Jeremy and Ben Donovan, this time both talking to the paper doll girls. They both look at us sort of sheepishly, but we just keep walking toward the large tent where tables and chairs have been set up for people to sit down. Dozens of people dressed all in black circle the room with trays filled with crab cakes and tiny quiches.

"There's Jillian," I say, spotting her near the entrance at back of the tent through which the serving people keep appearing and disappearing. We thread our way through the crowd, navigating the maze of people and tables, but by the time we reach the back of the tent Jillian is gone. A gust of wind makes the tent flaps flutter. We peek through the opening. The makeshift kitchen is filled with half a dozen chefs in white coats and checked pants, working grills and wielding pastry bags. A long table is set up along one end of the kitchen, where more serving people are filling trays with different canapés and shot glasses filled with something bright green.

"Piper," Claire says softly, putting her hand on my arm. She nods toward the other side of the tent, where piles of coolers and empty metal pans are stacked. Sitting on one of the coolers is Charlie. His hair is hanging forward, covering his face. Across from him on another cooler is his dad, Frank. Claire and I stand, watching as Charlie reaches out and puts a hand on his father's shoulder. Frank looks up at him. I gasp when I see his face. He's a wreck. His cheeks are flushed and his eyes are red, bloodshot. Jillian sees us standing there and motions for us to leave.

"We should go," Claire says, pulling my elbow. We turn to walk out of the kitchen. Unfortunately I turn just in time to come face to face with one of the servers who is headed back into the kitchen to refill his tray. The good part is that it isn't one of the drink trays with the dozens of empty glasses; the bad part is that even an empty tray can make a lot of racket when it's knocked to the floor. I apologize, trying to step around the server, who is stooped to pick up the fallen tray. I look back to where Charlie is sitting with his father. I know I shouldn't, but I do. And while his father is sitting with his head in his hands again, Charlie is looking up. And he's looking straight at me.

I follow Claire out into the garden, where the servers have ditched their trays and are now busy moving all of the paintings into the big tent. Because instead of the sky just threatening rain, it looks like it actually *is* going to rain. I see Jillian's mother flitting around the garden, directing the servers and guests to head indoors. Claire and I stop under one of the blooming dogwood trees near the fountain.

"He looks terrible," I say, not sure whether I'm talking about Frank or Charlie.

"Yeah," Claire says. "I had no idea."

I shake my head. "Me neither," I say, but memories tug at me. Frank's increasing antisocial behavior and Charlie's general sadness.

"Hey, ladies," Jeremy says, walking up to us. "What do you say? You want to head indoors or do you want to stand out here and get soaked?" Ben Donovan is still talking to one of the paper doll girls. She keeps touching his arm while he talks. A voice on a microphone inside the tent announces that the auction is ready to begin. I peek through the open flap and see Frank standing next to Dorian on the stage. He looks wobbly, but okay. He's donned a pair of sunglasses that, while very odd—considering it's nighttime and he's inside a tent—can maybe pass for simple artistic eccentricity. Jillian walks toward us. Charlie is close behind her.

"So," Jillian says, brightly. "Can you believe it's going to rain? My mother is freaking out." I imagine she is freaking out, I think, but I'll bet it's a lot more because her artist is a wreck than about the state of the weather. Charlie won't meet my eyes. "Do you want to stick around for the auction or . . . Wait, where's Ben Donovan?" I gesture over to where the paper doll is pulling on his arm to get him to bend down low enough to let her whisper in his ear. Jillian looks mad, but Charlie looks like he's about ready to explode.

"You're here *with* Ben Donovan?" he says, turning to me. His voice is tense, each word clipped.

"Yes," I say.

Charlie smirks. "Figures," he says.

"What's that supposed to mean?" I ask him.

He turns back to me. "Why are you *here*, Piper?"

"I don't know. It sounded like fun," I say, getting angry myself. If I had to pinpoint exactly why I was getting angry, I wouldn't be able to. All I know is that I can't figure out why Charlie is so clearly furious with me and so not angry with anyone else. We hear Frank's voice over the microphone. It's loose and slow, but unless you knew what his voice usually sounded like, you wouldn't notice anything different.

"So," Jillian says again. This time the brightness in her voice sounds even less real. "Do you want to go in? Auctions can be pretty fun to watch." I keep looking at Charlie, who is alternating between glaring at Ben Donovan and me.

"I think maybe I'll see if I can get a ride home," I say.

"You sure?" Jillian asks. "It could be fun." Claire puts a

hand on her arm. Jillian looks at me for a long moment.
"Well, if Ben Donovan can't take you home, I'll get the
driver to take you."

"Listen," I say. "Thank you. This really was fun." She gives
me a hug, followed by Claire. Jeremy raises his hand and half
smiles. Only Charlie doesn't say anything. He just stares past
me, like I'm already gone. He turns and walks away. I notice
Jillian doesn't follow. "Okay then," I say.

I turn and walk toward Ben Donovan, who is typing into
his phone as the paper doll talks to him. I catch the end of her
phone number as I walk up. "Can you take me home?" I ask.

"Now?" he asks, looking up at me. I notice he has the
decency to look at least partly embarrassed about being
caught scamming another girl's phone number while he's
supposed to be with me.

"I really need to get home," I say.

"Of course," Ben Donovan says. I glance over toward the
tent entrance. Claire and Jillian both smile at me. I smile back
as I wait for Ben Donovan to say good-bye to the paper doll.
She does look slightly contrite for trying to snag my date. I
look back over, hoping to see Charlie again, but he's gone.
Jillian is leaning toward Jeremy to say something. He nods
and laughs. She smiles up at him as he reaches out to brush
her hair away from her cheek. Claire's not even looking at
them. She's looking at her phone and smiling as she types.

I follow Ben Donovan out to his car. He opens the door
for me. I climb in carefully, not that interested in embarrass-

ing myself further by giving everyone in the parking lot a look up my dress. He closes the door behind me and jogs around to his side. He climbs in, looking at me briefly. I give him the directions to my house and then lean my cheek against the window and close my eyes. I suddenly feel tired way down in my bones. The glass feels cool against my cheek and it makes me think about riding in Charlie's car. This thought just makes me feel more exhausted, like the last bit of air escaping from a balloon.

We ride in silence all the way to my house. Ben Donovan pulls up to the curb and jogs around the car to let me out, clearly anxious to be rid of me and my weirdness. I squeeze his hand and thank him for the ride at the curb, not wanting to deal with more awkwardness should he decide to walk me to the door. He seems relieved as I turn to walk away. I notice that he barely waits until I have the door open before he pulls away. The sky finally opens up. The rain is slow and gentle at first, but increases in intensity as I stand there. I turn and head inside. I shut the door and lean against it for a moment.

"Piper's home!" yells Dom from the living room. He runs around the corner, but stops short when he sees me standing there. "You look funny," he says. Lucy runs up behind him.

"You look beautiful," she says. "Like Cinderella." I smile at her, although I think she'd be pretty disappointed at the direction my fairy tale is going.

"I hate princesses," yells Dom, running away from me. Lucy chases after him and they disappear upstairs. I walk into the living room, where my mother is just hanging up her cell phone. She looks sort of sheepish, making me wonder what she's been up to.

"You do look beautiful," she says. She looks at her watch. "You're home a lot earlier than I thought you'd be. I was thinking eleven. Maybe later."

"Well, I didn't want to turn into a pumpkin," I say.

"Did you have a good time?" she asks.

I take a deep breath. "It was—" I try to finish the sentence, but can't. My mom looks at me.

"You okay?" she asks.

"I'm not sure," I say. I see the look on her face. "I'm just really tired." She doesn't look convinced. "I promise." She keeps looking at me, but she can't find anything. After all, it isn't a lie. I am tired. Really tired. "I'm going to get in bed," I say. She gives me a hug. I climb the steps slowly. I kick off my shoes and unzip my dress, careful to hang it up in my closet. I pull on a T-shirt and a pair of pajama pants; these have conversation hearts all over them. The one on my right knee says DO U LUV ME? I frown at it and click off my light. I climb into bed and lie there for a long time, waiting. I tell myself I'm waiting for sleep, but if I have to be honest I'm waiting for something else. A loud noise on the roof above me.

chapter eighteen

Hours later, I'm still trying to sleep. Finally I hear a car pull up in front of our house and a lot of doors opening and shutting. I walk to the window, hoping to see Charlie. What I do see is Jillian's mom shaking Frank's hand and him smiling slightly. She doesn't seem freaked, which is good. But, I also see Jillian talking with Charlie, then him bending down to hug her. I pull back from the window before I see anything else. I hear the car pull away as I climb back into bed. I'm sitting here arguing with myself about whether I should go over and talk to Charlie or not. I check the clock—almost one in the morning. I think probably not. I lie back down and try to sleep again. Finally I give up.

I sigh and pull my sweatshirt off my chair and yank it over my head. I open my window and gasp at how cold it's gotten. I climb through the window and onto the roof, being extra careful because it's still damp from the rain. I do make some noise though. Enough that if Charlie wants to talk to me, he'll know I'm here, but not so much that if he wants to ignore me, he can't. I sit for a long time feeling the dampness soak into my pajamas. I stare out at the night. I'm just about to give up when I hear Charlie's window sliding open. He climbs out onto the roof and walks part-way over and sits down. Usually we're within a few inches of each other. Tonight he's keeping his distance, even staying on his own roof instead of coming over to mine like he usually does. We stay like that, not really sitting together, but more like parallel sitting, for several minutes before he speaks.

"I just ate half a jar of peanut butter and a whole can of Pringles," he says. I smile into the darkness. We're both quiet as if weighing the nutritive value of his meal, but then he speaks again. "I didn't know you were dating Ben Donovan."

"Yeah," I say. "You sound surprised."

"I am," Charlie says.

"Why? Didn't think Ben Donovan would go for a girl like me?" I say it as a joke, thinking he will laugh, but he doesn't.

"I didn't think you'd waste your time on a guy like him," Charlie says.

"He's nice," I say, defensively.

"I didn't say he wasn't."

"You implied—"

"Piper, I merely said—"

"Charlie, I didn't come out here to talk about Ben Dono-van."

"What do you want to talk about, Piper? The weather?" He laughs, but it's short and brittle.

"How's your dad?" I ask.

"Frank? Well, he's asleep right now. I'll tell him you asked about him."

"Why are you so angry at me?" I ask. "I didn't—"

"Didn't think? No, you didn't Piper. Maybe you should have thought that I might not like you surprising me to-night."

I shake my head. "I thought you liked surprises now. That's what you told your girlfriend."

"My *girlfriend*?" Charlie sighs. "I thought Jillian meant she made me cookies or something. I didn't think she meant that you were all going to show up and watch my dad make a fool of himself."

"Charlie. He was fine. I don't think anyone noticed."

"It's not *anyone* I was worried about. It was *you* noticing."

"Your dad was a wreck. So what?" I look over at Charlie, but he's turned away from me. "I'm sure he was nervous. Frank's not the most social person. I imagine being up on a stage with a bunch of Atlanta socialites looking at him is pretty much Frank's biggest nightmare." I pause, waiting for him to say something. He just keeps looking straight for-ward. "Listen," I say finally. "It was just one time. It's no big deal."

"Piper," he says, finally turning to look at me. "It wasn't just tonight. It's all the time. Since my mom left, he can't sleep. He can't eat. He barely paints. It's like living with a ghost."

"I didn't know—You didn't tell me." I stare out into the night in frustration. "How can I help you if you don't tell me what's going on?"

"I didn't ask for your help," Charlie says. The darkness makes it impossible to see his face. He takes a deep breath. "Anyway, I'm fine, Piper. You worry too much."

"Charlie, why are you doing this?" I ask. "Why are you pushing me away?"

Charlie laughs, but it's hard and sharp, like broken glass. "That's pretty funny coming from you."

"What are you talking about?" I ask. I shove my hands into the pocket of my sweatshirt.

"You are the queen of pushing people away. Beau, your friends, pretty much every guy you've ever dated." He pauses. "And me."

"I don't—"

"You do, Piper." He says it softly.

"You don't know anything about me," I say. I turn to go back inside, but his voice stops me.

"I know you better than you think," Charlie says. I turn and stare at him. "I know your heart is still broken from when your dad took off. I know you pretend you're mad at Beau because he left your mom, but you're just as mad that he left you."

I breathe in and out.

"I know the few times you've dated anyone, they're guys who will never even come close to understanding you. And even then you still figure out a way to dump them before they can get to know you."

"That's not true—"

"I know that you want someone to love you, but you're afraid to love them back."

"You don't know anything," I say. My cheeks are hot and my hands are shaking. "Just leave me alone." I inch back down toward my window.

"Piper, stop pushing *me* away," Charlie says.

"Or what?" I ask. "Or you'll go away?" I turn and stare at him, daring him to disagree.

He shakes his head. "I was just going to say that when you push me away, it hurts." I climb back through my window and shut it behind me. I change my pajama pants, leaving the damp ones balled on the floor. I get into my bed and stare at my ceiling. I don't hear anything for a long time, but finally I hear Charlie stand up and go back inside. I'm not sure what scares me more, the fact that he waited out there so long to see if I'd come back out or the fact that he finally gave up and went inside.

I did finally fall asleep, but it wasn't nearly enough. I'm still exhausted. I pretty much half slept through all of my classes, which can't be good for my GPA. I saw Ben Donovan twice in the halls, but he just sort of half waved at me and scooted away, making me think: *I am now the girl who made Ben Donovan have the worst date of his life.* The rest of Wednesday rolls right into Thursday with too much work, too little sleep, and silence from Charlie. By the time the final bell rings on Thursday, I'm ready to drop, but I stop by Jan's hoping he'll send me home. Unfortunately, he's so busy that I have to stay.

Jeremy and I fill the empty jars with jelly beans and gummy bears and peppermints. He tells me about the auction and about how happy Jillian's mom was with the turnout, despite the bad weather. I ask him if it was weird for him to see Jillian and Charlie hanging out at the Umlaut thing.

"Did you take your stupid pills this morning?" Jeremy asks me.

"What are you talking about?" I ask. Jeremy shakes his head and walks away from me. Jan comes out of the kitchen, wiping his hands with a towel. He looks nearly as tired as I feel. Ever since the Food Network vans left, the store's been mobbed.

"I just can't keep up," he says. "I can't make enough candy to keep the cases full. We're out of nearly everything."

"Welcome to the big time," I say, funneling Consternation Hearts into a new box. I close the flap and start on the next one. "Good thing you're expanding," I say.

"What?" Jan asks. He's staring at the menu board, trying to figure out what to erase. "Oh yeah, that."

"I saw that they took the *For Lease* sign out of the window." Jan nods and wipes "Bacon Truffles" off the board. Jeremy has been churning them out, but people keep buying them faster than he can make them.

The door to the shop bumps open. It's Jillian. "Hey," I say.

"Hi, Piper." She seems nervous and weird. And I wonder if she's worried about seeing Jeremy, but when he walks through the door from the kitchen it isn't weird at all. Apparently she's only weird with me. Great. I keep filling boxes of candy hearts, one after the next like I'm some sort of machine. When I run out of candy, I go back to the kitchen to get another case. Jillian, Jan, and Jeremy are all standing around the island, talking, but they get quiet when I walk in. I just head past them and grab another bin and push back through the door to the shop. I keep filling boxes in between customers, filling until all of the hearts are gone.

A woman in a red hat comes in with one of our bags in her hand. "Hi," she says. "I bought these a little while ago." I nod, wondering if I look stupid or something. I was the one who waited on her less than an hour ago. "Anyway, I was talking to one of my girlfriends over coffee. You know at that little shop down on the corner." I have to resist the impulse to make the hurry-up-with-the-story motion that Jeremy always makes. "I wanted to show her how clever your candies are." She pauses.

"Well, thank you," I say.

She looks at me for a moment. "Well the thing is . . . and

I'm sure it was just an oversight . . . there wasn't any silver heart in there. And see . . . I checked all of them and none of them has one." Jan comes out of the kitchen with a big tray of truffles in his hands. He puts them on the counter beside me and smiles at the woman before starting to refill the case. I look back at the woman, who is just standing there looking at me and waiting.

"What?" I begin. "I mean, I'm sorry, but I—" Okay maybe I am stupid. I have no idea what she's talking about.

"It's no problem," the woman says. "Maybe you could just give me the silver hearts. I can put them in the boxes myself."

"I just—"

"Of course," Jan says. He reaches under the counter for a cellophane bag. He opens a box under the counter and pours a handful of silver fortune hearts into the bag. He twists the top closed and hands it to her. "I'm very sorry," he says. "Here." He grabs another bag and drops two of his mood ring pops into it. "On the house." She's so happy with Jan that she just starts babbling all kinds of things at him. I sigh and walk back toward the kitchen to return the now-empty bin. Jeremy and Jillian are standing close together. She's saying something softly to him and he's rubbing her arm. When they see me, they both seem guilty. I just walk past them without saying anything. Maybe I did take my stupid pills this morning, because suddenly the entire world seems way too hard to understand.

I walk back into the front of the shop. Jan stops fiddling with the boxes of Consternation Hearts and looks up at me. He looks guilty too. "Okay, I'm sorry if I'm a little slow today, but what was that woman talking about?" Jan starts to say something, then stops and takes a deep breath, letting it out slowly. "Arrrghhh," I say, walking back around the counter and out into the café. I poke at the jukebox and the arm reaches in and selects one of the records from the row. (Yes, it's one of *those* jukeboxes and yes, it's worth a kazillion dollars, not that Jan would ever think of selling it.) "Moondance" comes spilling out of the speakers. Jan walks up beside me and looks in at the record spinning. "You going to tell me what's going on?" I ask.

He sighs again. "Which part?"

I laugh. "There are multiple parts?"

Jan laughs too. "Yeah, but I can't tell you all."

"Of course you can't, Yoda. You're about to tell me that some things I have to find out on my own."

Jan laughs again. "No, it's just that some parts aren't mine to tell."

"Could you be more vague?" I ask. Jan elbows me. "Just start with the red hat woman."

Jan adjusts his glasses and turns away from the jukebox. He leans back against it. I do the same. "I guess it's what I told you before, Piper. I just can't be that cynical about love. And I don't want you to be either." He pauses and pulls his glasses off and polishes them with the hem of his shirt. He puts his glasses back on and looks at me. "I just wanted to give people a little hope," he says.

"So you added one of your fortune hearts."

He nods. "I made them special for your Consternation Hearts."

"What do they say?" I ask.

He sighs. "The outside has 'Hope' printed on it and the inside says 'Believe in Love.'"

"Do *you*?" I ask. "Do you believe in love?"

Jan readjusts his glasses, stalling. "Piper, I was married for a long time to a woman I loved very much. Then I messed it up. I mean, it wasn't all my fault, but a lot of it was. You know?" I nod. I don't know, but I can imagine. "It took me a long time to forgive myself for all of that. A long time to believe in much of anything anymore. But you know what brought me back?" I shake my head. "Love."

"Love?" I ask.

He nods. "Powerful stuff."

"Whose love?" I ask.

"Well, my daughter's for one. My love for her and her love for me. And my ex-wife's. She's shown me a lot of grace over the years. Some good friends. Some great kids that seem to like hanging out with an old guy like me for reasons I can't begin to guess." He smiles over at me again. "See, the thing is Piper, it's really the only thing that's worth living for."

"Love," I say.

love? maybe. ♥

"Yep," he says. "How's that for Yoda?" I shrug. He takes a deep breath. "People are going to fail you in life. Sometimes in little ways. Sometimes in big ways."

"That's not exactly hopeful," I say.

"And you're going to fail others."

"Again, not that hopeful."

"Real love isn't bothered by that." He smiles at me. "When you really love someone, you see all their mess and their brokenness and you love them anyway. In fact, seeing all of that sort of makes you love them more."

I sigh and try to put words to a question that's been floating around inside my head for a long time. "What if you do that? What if you show someone who you really are and they don't love you? Or worse, they turn away like you're too ugly to love?"

Jan looks over at me. "I know you aren't talking about Piper Paisley. She is definitely not too ugly to love. She has all kinds of people who love her."

I sigh and shake my head. "Not everyone."

"Well, no," Jan says. "I mean, you can't *make* someone love you. Some people just don't have it in them or they don't want to. Some people are more interested in protecting themselves than in loving people." I nod. "And I don't blame them. I mean, hearts are delicate things."

"They are," I say.

"But they are also amazingly resilient," Jan says. I nod, thinking of my mother and Claire and now Jan. "So, that's it," he says. "Lecture over." He pushes away from the juke-box. "So what about you, Piper?"

"What about me what?" I ask.

"Will you at least think about what I said?" I nod. "Then my work here is done." He looks around at the shop. "Man, there is a lot of work to do," he says, laughing. I stay there, leaning against the jukebox. Maybe Jeremy's right. Maybe I'm not all that smart. It's like the whole time I've been focusing on my own brokenness, I've missed a very important fact. Everyone's broken. My mom, Beau, Jan, Charlie's dad. I think of the phone call I need to make. Even Jack.

The bells on the front door jingle. I look up and see Ben Donovan coming through the door. He looks around the shop for a moment, and then his eyes settle on me.

"Hey," he says. I smile at him. "Can I talk to you?" I nod and push away from the jukebox. I follow him outside where we sit at one of the tables. He looks past me for a moment then right at me. "Listen," he says. "I didn't want to just leave things between us like they were. All—"

"Weird?" I ask. He nods. "Ben," I say, aware that this is the first time I've ever said his first name by itself. "We're good." He smiles at me.

"Friends?" he asks.

"Only if you mean it."

"Paisley, I would be crazy to not want to be friends with you. You are one very interesting girl."

"I choose to take that as a compliment," I say, laughing. I

see Charlie's car pulling into the lot, then him climbing out. He sees me sitting there and pauses, but then keeps walking toward us. He nods at Ben when he walks past, but barely acknowledges me. He walks into Jan's shop, letting the door whoosh shut behind him.

"So we're good?" Ben asks.

"Definitely," I say. Ben stands up and pulls his sunglasses out of his pocket and puts them on.

"I'll see you at the meet tomorrow," he says. He starts walking toward his car, which is parked at the other end of the lot past Charlie's.

"Wait!" I say. "Are you the one who's been putting stuff in my locker?"

"What are you talking about?" he asks.

"Nothing," I say.

He smiles and shakes his head at me. "Hey, try not to puke in the pool during the meet. Okay?" I start laughing. I watch him climb into his car and pull out. *I am now the girl who is friends with Ben Donovan.* My phone moos in my pocket and I pull it out. There's a text from my mother.

Jack called again.
I love u—M

Below there is a number, which I assume is Jack's. I take a deep breath. Might as well, I think. I dial the number, remembering what my mother said about the octopus. A woman answers. I ask if I can talk to Jack. She asks who's calling. When I tell her, she gets quiet, and then she tells me to hang on. I look at the clouds drifting overhead as I wait.

"Hello?" It's my father. I take a deep breath.

"Hi," I say. "It's Piper. Mom said you wanted to talk to me."

Jack clears his throat. I hear a woman laughing in the background and then the sound of at least two kids laughing with her. "I appreciate you calling." It sounds so formal, like we don't even know each other, which I guess we don't. He's quiet for a long time. "Piper—I don't know how to exactly—" He pauses. "Listen," he says finally. "I've been a really terrible father to you." I resist the urge to say anything. I mean, what can I say? "I was hoping—" He gets quiet for a long moment. "I mean, only if you want to—" He laughs a little. A nervous habit we share. "Piper, what I mean to say is I'd like to know you."

"Why now?" I ask. I'm not angry. Just confused.

Jack sighs. "I guess I finally just got up the courage to ask."

"I need to think about it," I say.

"Of course," he says. I hear the sadness in his voice. "I just wanted you to know I'm here if you—" He breaks off again. Neither one of us says anything for several moments. Then he breaks the silence. "Maybe we'll talk soon," he says.

"Yeah," I say. I put on my sunglasses because I can feel the tears coming. "I should go," I say, finally. I listen to him say good-bye and then the click of him hanging up.

Instead of holding back the tears like I've done so many

times before, I just let them fall. Big fat tears that hit the top of the stone table, making wet patches. I hear the door to Jan's open and I look up. Charlie stands there looking at me. He starts to say something, but I just shake my head. I can't really deal with anything else at this very moment. I stand up and walk away from him toward the end of the block, where I turn the corner. I stop and lean against the stone wall, just feeling the cool rocks on my back. I cry until the tears finally stop, like I've just run out. I stand there for a while longer before I walk back around the corner and toward Jan's. Where Charlie's car was parked is a big red Hummer. I walk into Jan's. He's standing at the counter talking on his cell.

"She's here," he says. "I will." He clicks his phone shut. "Your mom," he says, putting it on the counter. "She was worried." I nod. "You okay?" he asks.

I take a deep breath. "I think so," I say.

Jan looks at me for a long moment. Then he smiles at me and claps his hands. "Well, good. Because there's a lot of work to do and I need the help."

"That's why you pay me the big bucks," I say. This makes him laugh. And when Jan's laughing you can't help but laugh too.

chapter nineteen

I'm washing dishes when Jan's car pulls up in front of our house. I look out the window over the sink. There's someone in the front seat with him, but I can't figure out who until he opens the door and the overhead light goes on. It's Jillian. Jan climbs out and walks around the back of the car toward the Wishmans'. Jillian climbs out of the passenger side. I figure she's going in with Jan, but I'm wrong. She walks up our sidewalk and knocks on the front door. I dry my hands on a towel as I walk to the door. I sling the towel over my shoulder and pull the door open.

She smiles slightly at me then looks away. "Want to come in?" I ask.

"Can you come out?" she asks. I walk through the kitchen, tossing the dish towel on the counter. I tell my mother, who's sitting in the living room with Dom and

Lucy, that I'm going for a walk. I walk out front and pull the door shut behind me. Jillian and I head down the sidewalk and toward the park at the end of our street. "I'm sorry," Jillian says.

"For what?" I ask.

She sighs. "Let's see. For The Plan. For the stupid love potion. For pushing you to go out with Ben Donovan—"

"We just call him Ben now," I say.

She smiles at me. "Mostly I'm sorry about all the mess with Charlie."

I walk over to one of the swings and sit down in it. Jillian sits in the one next to me, facing the other direction. I push off a little, making myself drift back and forth slowly. "So, you like Charlie, huh?" I'm not sure what else to say. Jillian grabs the chain on my swing and twists me to look at her.

"You're serious, aren't you?" I nod. She smiles and then starts laughing. She's laughing so hard she has tears in her eyes.

"I'm not sure I see what—"

"I know," she gasps. "That's the worst part of it. You don't see—" She takes a deep breath and looks back at me. "I don't *like* Charlie. First, he's, well, he's Charlie, and second, you saw me with Jeremy. I love nerds and Jeremy is about the nerdiest nerd of them all. You know what he bought me for Valentine's Day?" I shake my head. "A star!" She starts laughing again. "One of those!" She points wildly toward the sky above us.

"Which one?" I ask, smiling.

"I know!" she says. Soon we're both laughing so hard that our swings are going back and forth without us having to push ourselves. "Wait, it gets better. I have a certificate." She sees my face. "It has a picture of my star on it. Well, at least I think it's my star. It's sort of blurry—"

"And far away." She starts laughing again, which only makes me laugh harder. I push off and swing back and forth, a little higher. Jillian swings too and for a moment our swings chase each other back and forth, then we get out of rhythm and we rush past each other.

"Jan said he talked to you," Jillian says. I look over at her, but the swinging is giving me vertigo, so I have to look away. "He's over at Charlie's talking to Frank now."

"About what?" I ask. "Getting some help?"

"Yeah," Jillian says. "He was telling Charlie about all sorts of things this afternoon. Apparently there are a lot more broken people around than I thought."

"I hope Frank listens," I say.

"Jan can be pretty persuasive," Jillian says.

"Pfft, Jan has nothing on you. Look how you got me and Claire to go along with The Plan," I say. "And that whole love potion thing you did for Claire? That was genius."

Jillian drags her sneakers in the dirt, slowing herself down. I do the same and we slowly drift together again. "I did that for *you*," Jillian says.

"Me?"

She laughs. "For such a smart girl, you sure can be stupid sometimes."

"That's what your boyfriend tells me," I say, thinking of Jeremy asking me if I'd taken my stupid pills.

"Look, I knew Claire would be fine. She just had to figure out what a loser Stuart was, which she did. And I knew she would be on to bigger and better things, which she is. It's you I've always been worried about." She looks up at the stars just starting to push their way through the clouds above us. "I just thought maybe you could use a little magic in your life. I thought maybe it would give you a little hope."

"Make me believe?" I ask. She looks at me and nods. I look back at the stars above us. "So which one do you think it is?" I ask.

Jillian laughs and looks up too. "That one," she says, pointing straight up. "The twinkly one."

"It's a good star," I say. We both lean back, hanging from our hands and letting our heads fall back so we can look way up. When you do that, it looks like the whole world is full of stars. Just millions and millions of points of light, twinkling for anyone to see. Anyone who takes the time to notice.

Suddenly Jillian grabs my hand and turns me toward her. "Thank you," she says.

"For what?" I ask, standing up

"For putting up with me. I know I'm too loud and too opinionated and too—"

I lift my hand. "You are," I say, "but you're also an awesome friend." Jillian stands up too and throws her arms around me.

"You know," I say as we start back toward my house, "having your own star is pretty awesome." She smiles at me. "It's like your own personal wishing star," I say.

"I'll share it," Jillian says. "You can make wishes on it anytime you want." I smile, but there's an ache in my chest. Suddenly I miss Charlie more than ever.

Jan's car is still there when we get back. We walk through the front door, shivering. We hear my mother laughing. We peek around the corner into the living room. Jan and my mom are sitting on the couch and he's telling her the shark story that I've heard a thousand times. The one about how he almost got eaten when he was out surfing. Each time he tells it, I swear the shark grows about a foot. She sees me and waves. I smile and shake my head. Jillian follows me into the kitchen. I fill up the kettle and turn the flame on under it to heat up water for tea.

"Is this one of the other things that I didn't see?" I ask.

"What?" Jillian asks.

I roll my eyes. "My mother is going to start dating Jan, isn't she?" Jillian laughs. I pull mugs out of the cabinet and set them on the counter. We hear my mother laughing again. "That is a good surprise," I say. We sit and drink tea, listening to Jan and my mother laughing until Jillian finally tells them that it's past her bedtime.

"It's pretty bad when we have to be the grown-ups," I say.

Jan just smiles at me and shakes his head. We all walk out on the porch. Jillian hugs me again.

"See you tomorrow," she says. She walks to the car and slides into the passenger's seat. My mother walks Jan all the way to the car.

"Keep it PG—there are minors present," Jillian says from the front seat. Jan and my mother just laugh. He walks around his car and climbs in. Mom walks back toward me, smiling the whole way. We head inside. She walks around humming and shutting off all the lights downstairs. I follow her upstairs. She kisses me lightly on the forehead before checking on the kids. She doesn't stop humming softly to herself the whole time. I head into my room and drop onto my bed. I don't hear her go into her room. I don't hear anything on the roof. I take a deep breath, letting myself sink into my pillow.

The sunlight is way too bright and morning is way too early. I'm pretty sure I've never felt as horrible as I do at this very moment. I lie down and then the room starts spinning, so I have to sit up, but then I get weak, so I have to lie down again. Mom called school and then my coach to tell them I wasn't going to be in classes or the meet. The office said they'd send my books home with Jillian and Claire, just so I didn't fall too far behind. It's awesome that they care so much.

I spend the entire day on the couch. It stinks to be all alone when you're sick, but at least it's quiet. I made my mom go to work. It's the day before Valentine's Day, the single busiest day of the entire year. I try to watch television, but all the moving colors make me feel dizzy. The food commercials are the worst. Just seeing someone breaking a chocolate chip cookie in half so we can all see the melty chocolate chips makes me feel nauseated. I lie back and pull the fleece blanket from my bed over my legs. I keep alternating between shivering like I'm out in a snowstorm and feeling like I'm a baked potato that's been left in the oven for too long. It's after three, so school's out and the swim meet's started. It's Beau's weekend to have the kids, so at least it will be quiet here.

I must have fallen asleep, because the next time I look at the clock it's nearly five. There's a knock at the door. Maybe it's just the UPS guy. I close my eyes, willing him to go away. I try to sleep, reasoning that if I sleep, maybe when I wake up it will stop feeling like I lost a bet with a semi truck. But the knocking starts again. "Go away!"

"Piper! It's me." I sigh. Beau. I push myself back up and walk to the door. I pull it open and lean against the doorjamb. "Mom's not here. She went into the shop." I look past him to his truck. "Where are the kids?" I ask.

"Stacy's playing hide-and-seek with them back at the house," he says.

I nod. "I have to sit down," I say, worried that if I don't *sit* down, I'm going to *fall* down. Beau follows me inside and over to the couch. I drop onto it and close my eyes again.

Big mistake. I push myself back to sitting. "I'm okay," I say, then laugh.

Beau laughs weakly too. "If this is okay, I'd hate to see you not okay. Listen, I was just worried about you here. All alone."

"Thanks," I say. "What's in the bag?" I ask, gesturing toward the paper sack sitting at his feet. He picks it up.

"Maybe things for when you're feeling a little better." He pulls out a big bottle of ginger ale and a bag of cheese Goldfish. "I know you like these," he says, placing them on the table. "Tell me what I can do," he says.

"Nothing. Really. I just need to rest," I say. I lie back down on the couch. Beau pulls a blanket over me.

"Piper," he says. "I know this isn't the best time—" I look over at him. He's looking down at his hands, which are folded in his lap. "I know I've made a lot of mistakes . . ."

I raise my hand. "We all have," I say. The cynical part of me wonders if it's Reconcile with Your Estranged Daughter Month or something.

"I'd like it if you'd let me take you to dinner sometime. Or the movies. Just us." I smile at him. "When you're feeling better."

"I'd like that," I say, and with those three words, I make up my mind about Jack too. Everyone deserves a second chance. "Now go. I'm sure Stacy's awesome, but you know how Lucy is. She's impossible to find and she always has the best hiding places." Beau smiles and I wonder if he's thinking of the time that we lost her for almost an hour because she hid herself in the back of my closet and fell asleep.

"You sure you're okay?" Beau asks. I nod. He's reluctant to go.

"I promise," I say. He squeezes my hand and stands up. I watch him walk to the door and pull it shut behind him. It clicks locked. I take a deep breath. Sleep. Please. Sleep.

My phone moos from where I left it on the kitchen counter. I look at the clock. It's now after six. The phone keeps mooing at me. I'm guessing my mother. If I don't answer it, she'll freak and probably have the police here to check on me. I get up and walk toward the kitchen, keeping a hand on something solid at all times. I pick up my phone and look at it. Claire. I start to say hello, but she's already talking and not to me.

"Hello?" I ask.

"Oh," she says too loud in my ear. "Piper, how are you feeling?"

I hear a rustling noise and then Jillian's voice. "Just let us in," she says. "We knocked, but you must have been asleep. You didn't hear us." I walk to the door. I pull it open, but I don't wait for them to come in, I just head back to the couch.

Claire comes in first. "Oh no," she says. "You look like—" Jillian elbows her. "Poor baby," Claire says, coming over to sit by me.

"Careful," I say. "I've got the plague." Jillian puts a stack of books on the table. I groan. It's a big stack, and big stack equals lots of homework. But then she puts something else on top. A brown paper bag. "What is it?" I ask. I look over at Jillian, who doesn't say anything. "Don't pretend you didn't look." She reaches in, pulls out something white, and unfolds it. She turns the T-shirt toward me. I laugh a little even though it hurts to do so. It says I heart you, but instead of the regular Valentine's Day heart, it's a picture of an actual heart, all veiny and squishy looking. "Ugh," I say. "Put it away." The picture of the heart makes me feel all throw-upy again. Jillian puts the bag with the T-shirt in it in the kitchen where I can't see it. "Aren't you going to tell her?" Claire asks.

"Which part?" Jillian asks, walking back over to where Claire is clearly about to come out of her skin with excitement. Claire makes big eyes at her. "Okay, we caught the guy putting the stuff in your locker." I raise my eyebrows. "It was Jeremy."

"What?" I ask. "Why? Don't tell me *he's* my secret Valentine."

Jillian shakes her head. "He was just the messenger."

"But he's not talking," Claire says. She smiles and makes big eyes at me, suggesting that he did, in fact, *talk*, but that they aren't going to tell me what he said.

"Well, it's for sure not Ben," I say. I tell them about talking to him at Jan's. I'm too tired to try and pry whatever Claire is hiding out of her. One question does occur to me. "How did Jeremy get my combination?" I ask.

e? maybe.

Jillian shrugs. "He works in the office during fourth period. He has access to all kinds of stuff." I close my eyes and lean my head against the back of the couch.

"Tell her the rest," Claire says.

"There's more?" I ask.

Jillian nods. "So we went to the swim meet after school." I nod.

"Just tell her," Claire says. Apparently she's too impatient to let Jillian tell the story. "Charlie started a fight with Ben Donovan and got kicked off the pool deck." I sit up fast. Bad move. I lean back again.

"We just call him Ben now," Jillian says.

"We do?" Claire asks. I make Jeremy's hurry-up gesture with my hand.

"Well, he didn't actually hit him or anything, but there was some yelling. Mostly Charlie. And then Charlie pushed Ben Donovan into the pool."

I shake my head. "Boys and sports."

Jillian snorts. "It wasn't about swimming, Piper. It was about you!"

"What?" I ask. Claire and Jillian both start nodding.

"Charlie freaked when he saw Ben Donovan. I mean, Ben. He yelled at him for making you cry."

"What?" I ask. "He didn't—" Then it dawns on me. "Oh," I say. I explain that Charlie saw me talking to Ben and then while he was inside I called my dad. Claire makes me stop and tell them that story. Then I tell them how the next time

Charlie saw me, I was crying. "But not about Ben. About my dad."

"Wow," Jillian says. "Poor Ben." She smirks when she says it. "First he gets dumped by you and then he gets shoved in the pool by Charlie. Ouch." Jillian and Claire stay for a while longer, trying to cheer me up by telling me more Montrose gossip.

Claire looks at here watch. "We should go," she says. She looks sheepish when she says it. "I'm sort of going to the movies with Alex." I raise my eyebrows at her, but she swats my leg. "Just as friends," she says.

"Does Alex know that?" I ask.

"I don't think Claire knows that," Jillian says. "But yeah, we should go. I told Jan I'd come by the shop to help him and Jeremy get set up for tomorrow. It's going to be huge." They let themselves out with promises *not* to call and check on me later. I tell them I need to sleep.

Mom comes home about seven and clucks around me for a while. Jan comes by soon after and basically drives me nuts too. He keeps hovering over me, asking if I want anything—another pillow, a glass of water, a cool cloth. Seeing them together makes me happy, but their combined parental energy is making me nuts. "Don't you two have somewhere else to be?" I ask. "Dinner? A movie?" I finally convince them to go out to dinner. I push myself off the couch and walk them both to the door, telling them that I will be locking it behind them and they will not be allowed back until eleven, at least. I push the door shut behind them and lean against it, afraid to walk back to the couch or rather afraid to *try* and walk back to the couch and end up just falling on my face. There's another knock before I even make it away from the door.

"Go away," I say. "I told you not until after eleven."

"You want me to come back after eleven?" a voice asks. It's not my mother and Jan. It's Charlie. I pull open the door and let him in. I walk back over to the couch, muttering under my breath, something about Grand Central Station. Charlie walks in and closes the door behind me. He has a plastic bag in his hands, which he puts on the table beside my stack of makeup work.

"Claire and Jillian dropped them off," I say, nodding toward the books.

"I'm sure they told you," he says. I squint at him. "About Ben Donovan," he prompts.

"You mean about how you are now the guy who picked a fight with Ben Donovan?" I laugh.

"Not really my finest hour," he says, shaking his head.

"You realize you did it for no reason," I say. I tell him about talking to my dad and explain that I was crying because of that.

"That information would have been useful *before* I shoved him in the pool." I smirk at him. "I got *removed* from the swim meet."

"Your coach kicked you off the team?" I ask.

Charlie shrugs. "It won't last. Coach likes to win too much to keep me off the roster for long. Plus even though he would never admit it, I don't think he was really upset that I took Donovan down. He just told me to do it *in* the water next time." I laugh, but then wince. My head is pounding.

"What's in the bag?" I ask. He picks it up and starts emptying the contents. He sets a bottle of ginger ale on the table. Then he pulls out a DVD and a pint of ice cream. I smile at the various things he's brought.

"What ?" Charlie asks.

"I told Jillian I was going to spend Valentine's Day on the couch with a pint of ice cream and a monster movie." For some reason that conversation feels like it was ten years ago. "But I don't really feel like ice cream right now," I say. "I'm sorry."

Charlie smirks. "Don't be. More for me," he says. "Anyway, it's not Valentine's Day yet. Not until tomorrow." He gets up and flips on the television and puts the DVD in the player. Then he goes to the kitchen and comes back with a spoon. He sits down beside me on the couch and pulls my legs into his lap. He pops the top off the pint of ice cream and scoops out a big spoonful. "You sure?" he asks me.

I wave my hand and close my eyes. "I'm sure," I say. "I don't think you want me puking all over you."

He smiles. "I appreciate that." He pushes the button on the remote and the movie starts. *Plan 9 From Outer Space.* I smile at him. "See? I do know you."

"You do," I say. He takes another bite of ice cream. We watch the movie for several minutes then I close my eyes.

"I didn't get to tell you, but you looked really pretty the other night."

"Thank you," I say. "Now I just look pretty awful."

"No," says Charlie. "You don't." I open my eyes and look at him. He's just watching the movie and eating ice cream, but his cheeks are pink. I smile and close my eyes. I'm not sure whether it's just the fever or something else, but I suddenly feel warm all over. I peek at Charlie again and I can sort of see what Jillian was talking about when she went on about how crush-worthy he is. But from where I'm lying on the couch, it's not so much his hair or how tall he is or how green his eyes are, it's more that he brought me ice cream and a space movie and is spending his Friday night hanging out with me on the couch when I'm sick instead of going out. He looks over at me and suddenly it hits me. Charlie. Of course. It wasn't Ben or Jillian leaving gifts in my locker. It was Charlie.

"What are you smiling about?" he asks. It's my turn to blush.

"Nothing," I say. Charlie is my secret Valentine? I smile into my pillow. Maybe Piper Paisley isn't so cynical after all. I guess I fall asleep because the next thing I know it's dark and Charlie's gone and my mom's trying to get me to go upstairs to bed.

"Did you have fun?" I ask as she leads me upstairs.

"I did," she says. "Jan's a very nice man."

"He is," I say, climbing into my bed. She pulls the covers up over me. She strokes my hair and I start drifting off.

"He really cares about you," she says.

"Who? Jan? Yeah, I know."

"Well, I wasn't talking about him, but yes, Jan cares about you a lot. I was actually talking about Charlie."

"Yeah," I say. "He does." My mother keeps stroking my hair and humming. Whether she's humming because she's happy or to help me fall asleep, I don't know, but it does the trick.

The next thing I know it's morning and I don't feel like I'm going to die. I lie in bed for a long time, just thinking, but then I get up and head downstairs. There's a note from Mom to call her at the shop and there are seven messages on my phone. Two from Jan, one from Beau, one from Jillian, one from Claire, one from Jeremy, and one from Charlie. They all say basically the same thing. They all want to know if I'm feeling better and to wish me a happy birthday. And even though I still feel weak and headachy and generally nasty, *I am* feeling better and the odd thing is it's a happy birthday. At least the best one I can remember in a long time.

chapter twenty

I leave the overhead lights off and work by the glow of the pink and red strands of Christmas lights that are still hung in the windows. I offered to come in and take down all the Valentine's Day decorations to make room for the huge chocolate bunnies and the giant sugar eggs that Jan has been working on for the last month. He's always months ahead of the calendar, carving marzipan pumpkins in August and twisting candy canes while everyone else is dressing up their houses with ghosts and spiderwebs. I stack the remaining boxes of Consternation Hearts together and put them into one of the empty bins. I hold one up and look at it. I feel a little sad. I'm pretty sure this will be the last box. Somehow they just don't seem that funny anymore.

Jack answered the phone when I called after breakfast. I basically told him the same thing I told Beau when I returned his call. I want to spend time with him—get to know him—but I want to take it slowly. This hopeful thing is going to take a little getting used to. His voice was happy on the phone, which made me smile. He suggested we take a cooking class together at We're Cookin'. It should be fun. At least it will be interesting.

I wrap the leftover lollipops in plastic and place them into the box. I do the same with the gummy hearts and the giant red and white snakes. (I still stand by my assertion that just because they're red and white doesn't make huge gummy boa constrictors romantic.) Some of the candy, Jan will melt down for other items, but most of it, he'll just put at the back on the clearance table.

It took some convincing to get Mom and Jan to let me come in here, but after spending nearly my whole birthday on the couch, I told them I just needed to get out and move around a little. Mom said they'd be back in an hour to get me. No arguments. On the way here, they told me "the big plan." Jan is still going to knock down the wall between his shop and the empty space next door, but he's not going to take it over. My mother is. She's going to move Lilly's Flowers into that space.

"It's perfect," Jan said. "Flowers and candy. What could be better together?" I was so thankful that neither of them said that the two of *them* would be better together, but even still I saw Jan squeeze Mom's hand. I groaned in the backseat, making both of them laugh. It's going to take some getting used to, having Jan in my life as more than my boss, but already I can see hints of how good it's going to be. He knows more about *Star Wars* than Dom and he's already planned a tea party with Lucy. But the best thing is seeing my mom so happy.

I unhook cupid from the ceiling. It'll be another year before we see his pink cheeks and wings. Even though he's supposed to be smiling angelically, I can't help but think there's a little ironic glint shining out from his eyes. I give him a poke before I wrap him in tissue paper. Then I put him in one of the long-term storage boxes that Jan will keep way in the back of the storeroom.

My cell phone chirps and I pull it out. A text from Claire.

Miss u.

Alex says hi.

Talk l8r?

Luv, C.

I smile and slide the phone back in my pocket. It's the third time she's texted me from her date. She tried to drag me to dinner with her and Alex, but other than having my fingernails pulled out with pliers one by one, I can't really imagine a more horrible night. Jillian is surprisingly silent, which means her evening with Jeremy must be going well. They stopped by my house earlier and I had to laugh. I didn't think anyone would ever be strong enough to overcome Jillian's personality, but Jeremy can put her in her place. And every time he did it, I saw them smiling at one another.

I take down the lights last, leaving them plugged in. I coil them on the floor into big pink and red O's. The only person I haven't spoken with is Charlie. I wanted to call him all afternoon, but I didn't want to intrude on his time with his dad. When I bend to unplug the lights, there's a knock at the door. With the lights in my eyes and the darkness outside, I can't see who's there. "We're closed!" I yell, but the knocking continues. I think of Jan's admonishment to not even *think* of opening the door and wonder if it's him, trying to trick me. I walk over to the door and look out the window. I still can't see very well, but I'd know that silhouette anywhere.

I unlock the door and pull it open. "Hey," Charlie says.

"Hey," I say, suddenly shy in front of him.

"Can I come in?" I step back and let him in, locking the door behind him. "I thought I might find you hiding out here."

"I'm not hiding," I say.

"Pipe, you're in a closed store in the dark."

"It's not totally dark," I say, pointing to the coiled pink and red lights still blinking on the floor.

"I don't blame you. You're famous now." I shrug, thinking I could go for a little less notoriety. "They'll be talking about you for years," he says. "You dumped Ben Donovan."

"Well, you pushed Ben Donovan into the pool," I say. He just smiles at me.

"How's your dad?" I ask finally.

Charlie shrugs. "He seemed good when I left. Better. He

said he thought it might be good if he talked to someone."

"That sounds promising," I say.

He nods his head. "I think talking to Jan really helped."

"Jan's pretty wise," I say.

"It's just nice not to be alone in it. Nice to have people help us with everything."

I tilt my head, watching him. "So you're okay?"

"I'm good," he says. "I'm hopeful."

"Hopeful *is* good," I say.

Charlie laughs. "I didn't think I'd ever hear Piper Paisley say those words," he says.

I nudge one of his feet with mine. "Quiet," I say. "I've decided that I've had enough of cynical." We don't say anything for a few moments. "Want to help me pack up Valentine's Day?" I ask finally. We both look over at the last few hearts hanging limply from the wall and the empty wires poking down from the ceiling.

"Is it over already?" Charlie asks.

I look at my watch. "Not quite yet," I say.

"Well, then there's still time," Charlie says.

"Time for what?"

"Close your eyes," he says. "And put out your hand." I do. Then I hear rustling as he pulls something out of his jacket pocket. He places something in my hand. "You can look." I open my eyes. It's a very familiar brown bag.

"It was you," I say. He smiles.

"Did you know it was me?" he asks.

"Not at first," I say. "I figured it out last night when we were watching the movie."

"You mean when *I* was watching the movie," Charlie says. "You were zonked out, snoring."

I swat his arm with my free hand. "I was sick," I say. He just smiles at me.

He nods at the bag in my hand. "Aren't you going to open it?"

I tilt the bag and peek into it and immediately start laughing. "Candy?" I ask. I pull the box out of the bag and open it. Inside, nestled in a puff of tissue paper is a big red candy heart ring. "It's a heart," I say.

"Well, I know you collect them," Charlie says, teasing me.

I put the ring on my finger and hold it up. The facets catch the twinkling lights, making it sparkle like it's a real gem. "It's beautiful," I say, smiling. Maybe hearts aren't so awful after all.

Charlie shrugs, but I can tell he's pleased I like it.

I tilt my head and look at him. "Why did you have Jeremy leave gifts in my locker?"

"He had your combination."

"I *mean*. Why did *you* do it?"

"I just remember how excited you used to be about your birthday and about Valentine's Day and I just wanted you to have something to look forward to." He won't meet my eyes, suddenly shy.

He walks over to the jukebox and bends to plug the cord

into the wall socket. He punches a button and soon the store is filled with Sinatra. Charlie walks back over to me and holds out his hand.

"Shall we? I mean, you already know that I am an awesome dancer."

I laugh and take his hand.

"So what's next?" I ask.

"How about dinner?" he says, making me laugh. Still Charlie. Always thinking with his stomach.

"I mean—"

He pulls back and looks at me. "I know what you mean," he says. "But it's just us. Now maybe we'll just be more us."

"More us," I say, trying it out.

"You know, more me coming to your house and more you making me cookies and more you coming to cheer me on in my swim meets and more you helping me with my chemistry homework."

"Sounds awesome," I say, my voice heavy with sarcasm.

Charlie laughs. "I know you love planning things, but I don't think you can plan this." He puts his arms around me. "I like you—"

"I know that," I say.

He pulls away from me so he I can see his face. "Piper, you are my best friend in the whole world." He smirks. "I think that shirt pretty much sums up how I feel about you." I glance down, reading upside down. I smile. Charlie hearts me.

We dance slowly as the lights twinkle and the music plays. When the song is over, we just stand together. I lean my cheek against his chest. "I'm still scared," I say. Charlie hugs me tighter. "What if you leave?" I whisper.

"What if I don't?" he asks. I look up at him smiling down at me. He pulls me to him again and we start dancing. There's no music, but it doesn't matter. I find myself humming and this time Charlie doesn't tell me to hush.

chapter twenty-one

It's Jillian's idea for all of us to have dinner together. Her vision was a triple date at Wink or some other fancy restaurant, but I convinced her that maybe a picnic might be more fun. We decided to have the least romantic, least Valentine's Day food possible. Anything red or pink or heart-shaped we ruled off-limits.

Jillian, Claire, and I agree to take care of the food and we assign the guys to take care of the entertainment. Too bad their idea of entertainment is throwing Frisbees for Charlie's dog to fetch. Of course none of us took into account that it was still technically winter. I stamp my feet to try to bring some circulation back into them. My boots leave imprints in the snow. "I still can't believe it actually snowed." I say.

Jillian rolls her eyes. "This isn't exactly snow." She kicks at the ground, exposing the yellow grass beneath.

It's Claire's turn to roll her eyes. "If we have to listen to your stories of blizzards and ice storms in New York one more time—"

"Sorry," Jillian says. She kicks at the snow again. "Even though it's about the wimpiest snowstorm I've ever seen, it's still pretty cool." We decided against canceling the picnic, figuring it sort of fit into the whole misfit Valentine's theme we had going. "Our snowman is pretty sad though." The three of us laugh at the knee-high snowman, his head threatening to roll off his shoulders at any minute. A snowball whizzes past us, hitting the tree just behind Claire.

"Oh it's on," Jillian says. She bends and packs a snowball in her gloved hands and sends it flying back toward Jeremy. Her aim is better than his. The snowball hits his shoulder before breaking apart. I figure it's enough to start Snowball War II, but Jeremy just grins at her.

I sit on the edge of the picnic table bench, trying to keep as little of me in contact with the cold metal as I can. I watch as Charlie launches another Frisbee in the air and Duncan, the world's ugliest and awesomest dog, tears after it. "Do you know what's funny?" I ask.

"What?" Claire asks, sitting down beside me.

I look over at her. Her cell phone isn't in sight. "Those three actually ate the chocolates we made."

"You're right," Jillian says, sitting down on the other side of Claire. "Wait, what are you saying?"

I laugh at the intensity of her voice. "What I'm not saying is that the potion worked."

"Good thing," Claire says. I smirk over at her. She's right. If the potion had worked, there's a good chance we'd be having a picnic with Stuart and Ben and some random guy Jillian was crushing on.

"Oh my goodness," Jillian says, jumping to her feet.

"What?" I ask. Jillian just shakes her head and hurries off toward the parking lot. I look over at Claire, but she just shrugs. I see a furry blur out of the corner of my eye. I brace myself for impact just in time to keep Duncan from knocking me to the ground. I scratch his ears, smiling at his goofy face. He gives me one huge lick then flops on the snow at my feet.

"Ew," I say, swiping at my slobbery cheek with my hand. I look down at Duncan. "No offense," I say. In response, he wags his tail harder. Charlie sits down beside me, so close our shoulders are touching, and Alex and Jeremy fall on what's left of the pretzels.

"Where did Jillian go?" Jeremy asks. Claire makes big eyes at him and shakes her head. Suspicious. I look over toward the parking lot and see Jillian walking toward us, carrying a cake with candles poking out of its top. She walks slowly to keep the flames from going out. Jeremy starts and soon everyone else is singing "Happy Birthday" to me. Very loud and very off-key. Jillian reaches us and holds the cake in front of me.

"Make a wish," Charlie says. I glance over at him before closing my eyes. I hear the clink of the tags on Duncan's collar, then feel a paw on my leg. My eyes fly open just in time to see Duncan take a huge bite out of the cake. "Duncan! No!" Charlie says, but it's too late. I laugh at the guilty look on Duncan's face as he tries to lick the blob of yellow frosting off his nose.

While the cake is a little mangled, the candles are still all in place and actually still lit. I try to think of a wish. Just two weeks ago, I probably could have listed a dozen things I wanted, but now I can't think of a single thing to wish for. I close my eyes again, take a deep breath, and blow out the candles.